Dissent

Book I of The Nexus

By Thomas Olbert

Phase 5
Phase 5 Publishing, LLC
PO Box 1595
Asheville, NC 28802
www.phase5publishing.com

First Edition February 2016
Copyright 2016 Phase 5 Publishing, LLC
Story Copyright 2012 by Thomas Olbert, Licensed to Phase 5 Publishing, LLC
Cover Art, Copyright 2013 by Ryszard Jalowy (a/k/a Richard Yalovy), Licensed to Phase 5 Publishing, LLC
Spiral, by Andrew Fitzsimon, courtesy of Openclipart
Editor: Rebecca Ledford

Phase 5 Elements: Another World 205; Gynogenesis 99; Culture Clash 212

Classification: Science Fiction. Another reality; cosmic construction; gynogenesis; culture clash; far future; chimerism; war; prison work camp; planetary government; advanced science; corporate exploitation.

Appropriate for Adults: Moderately Explicit Violence and Death, including domestic violence; Brief explicit same-gender sexual situations; Profanity; Violence against and death of animals

ISBN 978-1-942342-89-2
More: www.phase5publishing.com
Printed and Distribution by Lightning Source, a member of the Ingram Content Group, in the United States of America.

Table of Contents

Preface

In the age before time...

The sapien species, in its original, unrefined form, destroyed nearly all of creation. Reckless use of new and untested technologies opened trans-dimensional gateways into unexplored universes whose physical properties proved incompatible with those of the home continuum.

The cosmic disaster which followed all but destroyed the sapien home universe, forcing what little remained of the species to migrate to another universe; a primordial universe where matter had yet to congeal into galaxies, stars or planets.

Over the millennia which followed, the remnants of the species elected to genetically weed out the evolutionary source of the demon whose insatiable hunger for conquest had brought forth the apocalypse. Males were rendered extinct, and forgotten. The femes who succeeded them created the Nexus, from which stemmed the web of cosmic strings forming the framework of a new universe. Having mastered time and space, the femes had unrivaled power over the future of a new creation.

But, what were they to do?

Prologue

The universe grew.

The cosmic web was spun wider and wider about the Nexus, the spirals of new galaxies forming in its embrace.

Ralyn entered the web link at the heart of the Nexus, and spread herself upon the winds of time as the quantum strain inside her stirred to life. Billions of genetically engineered microbial creatures that thrived in quantum space, they were as one with others of their kind moving through time and space along the cosmic strings.

Ralyn's bio-rhythms synched, in perfect symbiosis with the quantum strain, her mind rode the web, along countless branching time lines. Eons flashed by as a multitude of suns lived and died around her. Ralyn watched with a loving maternal pride as the alternate futures of her genetically engineered descendant races opened before her like the pages of a book...

She saw future worlds of beautiful floating cities where graceful winged femes bravely fought monstrous feathered serpents which carried their gestating young within.

Worlds of orbiting space colonies of dome-enclosed hydroponic gardens and agraria where beautiful, green-skinned, golden-eyed femes grew like flowers from pods and heroically battled horrific carnivorous plants to claim their young.

Worlds of blue oceans and underwater cities where femes evolved in a single life-span from land dwellers to amphibians to ocean creatures with gills and webbed fingers and silver scales glistening in ocean waves. They battled ebony reptilian demons that turned into sea serpents who carried their unborn daughters in eggs.

Space shimmered like summer heat as time raced on through the millennia, art and science evolving into patterns more terrifying and beautiful than anything Ralyn could have imagined. Yet, somehow...never the right combination of basic drives or adaptations to yield the desired evolutionary effect.

A sudden shift into murky darkness, a familiar, unsettling jolt of light, and she found herself back in the Nexus. She sank to her knees and fought off a wave of nausea as the quantum life-strain died within her. She sighed, brushing aside a tear.

Slowly straightening herself, she walked stiffly out of the web link chamber. She climbed into a transport module, strapped herself in and sealed the glass hatch of the cocoon-like pod. "Genesis level, Section R-12," she recited in a fatigued, scratchy voice, instructing the computer. She closed her eyes, her muscles tensing. She was thrust back against the cushioned seat as the module rocketed through the labyrinth of pneumatic tubes honeycombing the superstructure of the Nexus. As the pod slowed and she felt her stomach settling, she opened her eyes and found herself in the birthing chamber of her progeny to come.

Stepping shakily from the transport module, she looked at her nascent daughters as they grew in cylindrical glass tanks of liquid, fed through artificial umbilical cords. The Nexus had combined Ralyn's DNA with that of other administrators It judged worthy to propagate the next generation of cosmic planners.

Dozens of them, all created from the genes of the chosen elite, she mused, looking down the rows of tanks. Just as her line had been created from the essence of the now-legendary Kestra and a hand-picked few of her contemporaries. Her heart drumming with fear, she drew a control device from beneath her robes and activated the gatherer robots. Like huge, humming silver bees with glowing sapphires for eyes, they shifted into phase with the Nexus's bubble of normal space and floated into the chamber on shimmering fields of magnetic force. Ralyn forced her fingers to keep steady as she guided the machines to their biocybernetic interface terminals behind the rows of artificial wombs.

Accessing the computer monitor program, she broke down the collected DNA samples from the three alternate futures she had just visited and incorporated them into the genetic matrix of her descendants. As she transmitted the signal ordering the robots to release their charges of collected genetic material into the fetal sapiens, she prayed to the Multiverse she would be able to complete her task before the Nexus realized what she was doing.

Ralyn, a voice boomed in her head. Her heart nearly stopped. The Nexus. Did It know?

Stay calm, she commanded herself, steadying her thoughts. "Ralyn acknowledging," she responded via the telepathic implant in her brain. She masked her fear with practiced skill, using a jumble of mundane thoughts to distract the Nexus. "What do you require?"

Come to the main junction immediately. We must confer.

"Received. I will arrive shortly. End communication." She hurriedly completed her task, deactivated the robots, purged the computer memory of the process, and established a facade of false genetic data to hide the truth from the Nexus. Her nerves were strained as she rode the shuttle pod to the main junction; the very core of the immense artificial intelligence which was the mind of the Nexus.

She stood at the center of a wide, shining black circle at the center of a chamber of brilliant white walls and long, tapering black triangles. A huge, humming black sphere hung in midair before her. *Report,* the Nexus Overmind commanded. The voice was like a thunderclap in her mind.

We have our god, as the primitives have theirs, she mused bitterly, never daring to voice such thoughts, or let her telepathic barriers slip. She extracted a memory link device from her robe pocket and placed it against the surgically implanted access contact at the base of her skull. Pressing a button, she triggered the memory upload from her own brain to the Overmind.

Negative viability confirmed on all three recorded experiments, the faceless super-intellect coldly intoned. *Kalthaar remains the only potential success. You will instruct all sections to concentrate their efforts there.*

She nodded. Many times she had traversed the timelines of Kestra's famous creation; the future where two opposite and irreconcilable means of sapien reproduction existed side by side. A god for the self and a god for the tribe, locked in eternal combat for the soul of each individual. A fascinating and sometimes terrifying world.

Ralyn looked up and gasped as the chamber she was standing in was transformed into a black void of spinning star fields. Fleets of star cruisers traversed the space between the planetary systems of Kalthaar's galaxy. In just four thousand years, the femes of that world had developed interstellar travel and colonized many planets. Planets that had become independent worlds, established their own colonies and empires, and fought each other for supremacy across a galaxy. "What of the other three experiments?" Ralyn forced her voice to remain cold and aloof, a mother's love for her children well hidden behind a façade of scientific detachment. She clenched her fists, agonizing seconds ticking by as she awaited the answer.

For the time being, they will be retained for further study.

She exhaled deeply, tension flowing out of her body.

But, be warned: do not expend valuable time or effort on their behalf. They will all eventually have to be destroyed to make way for the future progress of the Kalthaar experiment.

She bit her lip until it bled, forcing a tear back from the corner of her eye. Tasting a bit of salty blood on the tip of her tongue, she dipped her head in a gesture of submission. "As you command." She said through clenched teeth. She had learned to maintain a mask of supplication with artful finesse, hiding the unspeakable hatred she felt for the Overmind.

Formed from the collected memory records and assimilated brain patterns of all preceding Nexus administrators since the time of Kestra, It had an intelligence that regarded her and her sister sapiens as a biologist might regard a culture of bacteria she was cultivating.

But, for all Its mighty intelligence, It was still only a machine; a series of extremely complex equations passing through a semi-organic cybernetic construct the size of a planetary system. It could calculate a billion possible futures for the entire sapien race in all its forms, and with unerring accuracy, but it could not muster a single nanosecond of compassion or imagination.

You are dismissed. The chamber walls blinked to a stark, featureless black.

She turned and strode out of the junction chamber, savoring her hidden knowledge; even if all else failed and the rest of her beloved children would someday have to be slaughtered, their beauty and spirit would live on in her daughters. *Someday, this monster will be destroyed*, she silently promised herself and all her children to come. *And perhaps*, she thought, daring to take a leap of faith, *The Kalthaar experiment may hold the key.*

Part I – Fleet Captain Kaylenn

Chapter 1

Timeline: Kalthaar Experiment
Timeline Spatial: The Planet Helkos in the galaxy of Kalthaar
Timeline Chronological: The fourth millennium after the age of Kaarth, section point 120794 (billions of years after Ralyn)

Kaylenn sighed as she stood atop the hill overlooking the spaceport. She had a fine view. Far beyond the gray steel decks, docking bays and transmitter towers, over the far hills beyond the jungle, Helkos Minor was visible, its silver-blue curve standing against Helkos Major's light blue sky, its largest moon, Kaarth, hanging overhead. A thunder-goddess class space destroyer was lifting off from the space port. The ground crews, their fueling operations complete, scattered like a tide of ants as the neutron boosters activated, and the gray-metallic juggernaut rose from her landing pad. The wind that fine bird of prey generated as she rose from the spaceport ruffled Kaylenn's long red hair and the folds of her uniform jacket. She smiled as she shielded her eyes against the triple red sun, watching the pride of the Helkos Confederation fly off to war.

"Fleet Captain, by your leave." The voice behind her was familiar. She turned. It was Neltryn, captain of her flagship, the *Kalthaar*. "The new teams are ready for your inspection, syr." The tall, attractive dark-skinned feme said, raising her fist in the traditional military salute of the space service. Her stance was firm and strong, as always. No trace of fear of what lay ahead. Kaylenn nodded with admiration.

"Very well," she said, returning the salute. "How do they look to you?" she asked her old friend and comrade.

Neltryn cast her large brown eyes about for a moment, then wet her full lips. "Competent. As well as could be expected for Kaltaarists, I suppose."

Kaylenn winced in disgust, turning back to the spaceport. She clenched her hand upon the ceremonial spear her late mother had bequeathed to her. The spear with which her mother had, twenty-five years earlier, killed a rival warrior and slain Krai, cutting the infant Kaylenn from the Mother Destroyer's womb and winning Kaylenn as her daughter. Since earning her first commission in the space service five years ago, Kaylenn had kept that spear as a good luck charm that had gotten her through six major space battles. The gold tassel and gold-trimmed banner of the Helkos Confederation fluttered from the spear shaft in the wind.

Daughter of a fine gathering, Kaylenn was, she thought with a mixture of pride and bitterness. Ten of the best warriors her home province had to offer. She could have chosen to rest on the laurels she was born with; her bloodline alone could have assured her a position of power in government or corporate service on the homeworld. But, she would have none of it. She had been determined to win her own place in the Confederation, as a warrior, like her mother. And, by every goddess, she had proven she had a soul to match her blood.

And now, after all her achievements, Fleet Command was sending her into galactic combat with Kaltaarists under her command! Was the war going that badly, she wondered with horror. Kaltaarists as warriors? What next? As political leaders? If not so obscene, and if so many people she held dear were not facing death on a dozen planets, the idea might actually have been amusing.

Neltryn nervously cleared her throat. Glancing at her wrist chronometer, Kaylenn saw time was short. No sense putting it off. "Let's get this over with," she said as she turned and walked down the slope of the hill, Neltryn beside her. As they walked toward their landed jet skimmers, Kaylenn had a passing fancy she decided to indulge. "Did you ever have sex with one of their kind?" she asked matter-of-factly, glancing over her shoulder at her subordinate.

"What, syr?" Neltryn asked, nearly stopping in her tracks.

"A Kaltaarist. Did you ever have one?"

Kaylenn hid a smirk behind false seriousness as Neltryn fumbled for an answer, obviously sweltering a bit inside her uniform. "Well...yes. A couple of years ago, I spent a furlough on one of their planets."

"Curious?" Kaylenn quipped as she climbed aboard her skimmer.

"A little, I guess," Neltryn muttered, tilting her head to hide a grin as she climbed aboard her own skimmer.

"And, are the rumors true?" Kaylenn asked, securing her spear beside one of the jet pods.

Her old friend looked at her and smiled. "They're adequate," she said quietly. "They have a fire for living, in their own way. But, they're a bit too...deferential for my taste, if you know what I mean."

Kaylenn nodded, starting her skimmer. She did know. She and Neltryn were much alike. And, if the demands and strictures of military command had not stood in the way, Kaylenn would have liked very much to have taken their friendship to the next level. The wind shrieked through Kaylenn's hair as she maneuvered her skimmer about ten feet off the ground, down the slope of the hill toward the spaceport, Neltryn keeping pace with her. *First rule of combat command*, she reminded herself as she set her skimmer down at a landing pad near the boarding ramps of her command cruiser. *Never get attached. The moment you allow favoritism to creep into your heart, you let your crew down.* And that meant death.

Her executive officer, Baltryk, and two ship captains stood at attention and saluted as she and Neltryn approached. "Progress?" she asked Baltryk.

"On schedule, syr," the tall, strong feme replied in her husky voice, a whisp of sandy hair blowing in the summer wind. "All sections report we're ready for liftoff, and the fleet reports we're on-track for rendezvous at designated orbital coordinates."

"Where are the new fighter crews?" she asked reluctantly.

"Formed up on the tarmac awaiting inspection, syr."

"Escort."

Baltryk saluted, and she and the other two officers led Kaylenn and Neltryn to a line of femes in space pilot uniforms standing at attention before a line of short-range space fighters. The traditional tattoo marks on their faces branded them all as Kaltaarists. This was the first time she had seen their kind on a military base as anything other than maintenance workers. She passed her eyes up and down the line. Their faces were frozen enigmas, but their bodies showed them for what they were; farmers, builders and laborers. Not a battle scar on any of them, nor that indefinable look that came with being a seasoned warrior. She looked at their eyes. Not a trace of eagerness or fear. Just calm readiness. She clenched her teeth, trying to hide her disgust. Was she expected to lead serving drudges into battle?

"Which of you commands this squadron?" she barked out.

One of them immediately marched forward in crisp

military fashion and saluted. "Saaryth, Lieutenant Commander, syr, at your command." Kaylenn looked her over. She was tall. Well-built. Attractive. Long, dark hair fastened in a military knot behind her head. Light brown skin. Large, striking dark eyes. A precision and discipline to her that was impressive. Kaylenn recognized the tattoo markings on her face as signifying membership in one of the Kaltaarist tribes of Trynn, a Helkan Kaltaarist world in the same star group as Kaylenn's homeworld, Zeln.

Kaylenn heard Neltryn's breathing accelerate just the tiniest bit. She glanced at her old friend and caught the briefest glint of anger in her dark eyes, just before Neltryn snapped her eyes straight forward and stood at attention. Jealousy? Was Kaylenn that obvious? No matter. Lust was an occupational hazard, and easily conquered. "You're from Trynn, Lieutenant Commander?" she asked, looking into the eyes of the Kaltaarist.

"Affirmative, syr."

"Your career there, before you were drafted into the service?"

"Respectfully, syr, my people do not have 'careers.' We have clan postings. Mine was spacecraft construction. I was head overseer of the fighter assembly section of the Trynn shipyards under military contract for the Vedran campaign. We produced the Taarex-class fighter deployed at the battle for the Quay-Len system. I myself tested all of the prototypes, from the Taarex to these Braal-class fighters my team will be flying on this mission." She inclined her head slightly, indicating the fighters lined up behind her. Kaylenn looked them over. Fine-looking birds. Formidable weapons. With the right pilots at the controls, anyway. "And, purely for the fleet captain's own information, syr, I was not drafted into the service. I volunteered. As did every feme in my squadron."

"Why?" Kaylenn asked point blank. "I thought Kaltaarists didn't believe in war."

"We do not, syr. However, as loyal citizens of the Helkos Confederation, we are beholden to the motherworld government for our protection. The planning commissions and tribal councils of our respective worlds have decided that, while some of us can better serve the Confederation as laborers and medics, others, like myself, are better suited to assist the war effort. The priestesses of Kaltaari counsel that each should serve the tribe in her own way, and according to her abilities."

"Yes, but surely you must feel morally compromised," Kaylenn said sarcastically, probing for a reaction. "After all, the killing of sister sapiens is considered an affront against that grazing beast you call a god, is it not?" The other feme's face remained as still and tranquil as a lake. She had not flushed. Her teeth had not even tightened. Was there no fight in these creatures?

"Once Kralites in their greed and violence insist on starting a war, there is nothing for Kaltaarists to do but try to ensure that they at least conduct it as efficiently and with as little useless bloodshed as possible."

Neltryn, looking angered, started to speak, but Kaylenn held up a hand to stop her. The flagship captain stepped back, looking frustrated. This Kaltaarist had bite, as well as a fetching frame, Kaylenn noted with a strange amusement. "Back in formation, Lieutenant Commander," she commanded. "You'll soon have the chance to prove just how efficiently you can run your squadron. Don't expect it to be like a simulator test."

"I will not, syr," she replied respectfully, saluting and marching back to her place with her pilots.

"Arrogant little work drudge," Neltryn grumbled as she walked with Kaylenn toward the *Kalthaar's* boarding ramp, her hands clasped tightly behind her back.

Kaylenn smiled slightly. "Tough, or completely ignorant," she said, the smile slipping from her face as she rubbed her fingers nervously against the shaft of the spear. "We'll find out soon enough."

Chapter 2

Timeline: Kalthaar Experiment
Timeline Spatial: The bridge of the Kalthaar,
interstellar space, en route between Helkos and the
Keltrys solar system in the galaxy of Kalthaar
Timeline Chronological: The fourth millennium after
the age of Kaarth, section point 120795

The ship trembled, metal bulkheads rattling as the laser batteries detonated several incoming robot bombs near the *Kalthaar's* hull. "Turn us toward them and bring the mains to bear!" Kaylenn shouted as her flagship faced off against the lead Vedran space destroyer defending the enemy fuel convoy.

"Yes, Fleet Captain," Neltryn responded, drumming instruction codes into her tactical board, her voice cool and steady. The *Kalthaar's* forward particle beam cannon fired streams of light into the darkness. Through her virtual reality headset, Kaylenn watched the computer breakdown of the hits scored on the enemy ship's forward armament. Scrolling text indicated damage, flashing blue circles indicating the sections of the enemy ship still protected by magnetic shielding. Hurriedly drumming the input keys on the panel of her command chair, she downloaded the tactical breakdown to Neltryn's terminal.

Kaylenn was nearly thrown from her chair by the next explosion to rock her ship. The bridge lights flickered wildly and alarm klaxons sounded as the enemy's barrage struck. Damage reports and casualty figures scrolled across Kaylenn's computer-generated display. "Twenty degrees hard a-port," Neltryn barked at her helm officer, processing the tactical layout and laying in a new attack vector. "Course zero-zero by seven zero four. P.B. turrets three, five, and seven fire at designated targets, on my signal only!" she said through her headset radio, feeding the target specs to her gun crews. Kaylenn admired her. She sensed Neltryn could command the obedience of her troops with nothing more than a change in tone. Kaylenn had chosen well for this war.

Kaylenn completed her plan by deploying robot bombs along the enemy ship's possible evasive routes and downloading their coordinates to Neltryn. The kill was set. "Number five, fire," Neltryn ordered. Kaylenn smiled as the computer registered a hit to the enemy's aft thruster section. "Number three, fire." Another hit, in the forward weapons array. Kaylenn salivated, savoring the thrill of the hunt. The damaged enemy destroyer turned and swung hard a-starboard, running. One of Kaylenn's robot bombs, sensing the enemy's approach, moved to intercept. The enemy fired their laser turrets, but Neltryn's aim had been good; most of their defensive laser array had been destroyed.

Smelling victory, Kaylenn removed her V.R. headset and switched the incoming data to bridge visual. It was time to reward her warriors with the sight of the enemy's blood, to fuel morale. The 'alert' signal flashed across a dozen monitor terminals. A dozen pairs of eyes snapped up. The decks, walls and overhead became a three-dimensional holographic projection of the enemy destroyer, huge and gray against the black and the stars. It was as if the forward section of the *Kalthaar's* bridge had suddenly been cut away, leaving the tactical, helm and radar officers sitting at their terminals staring into open space.

The robot bomb exploded against the destroyer's central gunnery tower, a flaming yellow sun erupting from the ruptured superstructure as the bridge section dissolved in white fire. "Number seven, fire," Neltryn ordered. The coursing blue-white energy stream of a particle beam hit the now-exposed fuel pods, triggering another explosion. The enemy ship flared like a nova and vanished into a ball of white light, the flash eclipsing the star fields for a moment. The bridge crew cheered wildly, shouting the ritual greetings used to honor the victor as she returned from the Great Hunt, the daughter of Kral in her arms.

"Well done, Neltryn," Kaylenn heartily declared. Neltryn looked up at her from her station and smiled, raising her fist in salute. "Now, let's finish the job. Take us to the convoy, and see if Baltryk needs any help with the rest of those destroyers. And, pick your targets carefully, Captain—we want the fuel convoy intact."

"Yes, Fleet Captain. Helm...new course: zero-seven by eight zero nine." Bits of still glowing ship debris spun past the *Kalthaar*, ripples crossing the holographic starfields as the occasional bit of flotsam struck one of the ship's magna shields. The ponderous gray and red bulks of the Vedran fuel tankers lined up bellow. Above, the battle raged. Destroyers and battle frigates maneuvered for control of the convoy, particle beam fire and exploding bombs lighting the blackness. Kaylenn drummed a few keys on her panel, overlaying the computer analysis onto the live-action visual.

Kaylenn's brows knotted. The enemy maneuvered well. The computer schematic showing the placement of red arrows symbolizing the enemy units and blue arrows signifying her forces left no doubt as to what the Vedran Fleet Captain had in mind. By arranging her ships in a crescent-like pattern, she was luring Kaylenn's ships into a clumsy central thrust while spreading her own fleet thinner and thinner along a lengthening curve. Once all of Kaylenn's surviving ships had taken the bait, she would close the crescent into a circle, cutting Kaylenn's fleet to bits. "Raise the *Braal*," Kaylenn ordered. "Put me in direct communication with

Captain Baltryk."

"Syr, there's no response on any com band," the communications officer said with a hint of nervous fear slipping into her voice as she looked at Neltryn with her slanted, dark eyes. "I get only static. They must be jamming us."

The dull, icy grip of fear touched Kaylenn's heart as she watched the visual. She instinctively grasped the shaft of her mother's spear, mounted in its base beside her command chair. "Deploy all robot probes!" she shouted. "Locate the *Braal* at once." Seconds ticked by, turning into minutes. Gunships exploded in flaring balls of orange fire, lighting up the convoy.

"Fleet Captain," the stocky little tactical officer said. "Probe Three has returned. Computer download confirms identification of the *Braal*. She's been hit, syr. Main section gone, bridge unit completely destroyed. No sign of escape pods or survivors. She's finished, syr."

Baltryk...dead? Kaylenn stared at the battle playing out before her...hardly a battle now, more like a leaderless pack of wild dogs chasing after prey, scarcely trying to avoid killing each other as they closed on their quarry. *Kral take the idiots!* she silently cursed, switching off the holographic display and donning her V.R. helmet. The Vedrans must have deployed some new jamming technology. Once Baltryk had lost contact with her attack group, order and formation had quickly broken down. The enemy fleet captain had played it perfectly, curse her. She had sacrificed a considerable portion of her fleet to take out Baltryk's ship. Once Baltryk was eliminated, every captain in her squadron was on her own.

Kaylenn choked in anger and disgust as she watched the haphazard strikes of a dozen Helkan ships chasing enemy cruisers that were obviously luring them to their doom. In her mind's eye, Kaylenn could see the captains in her fleet. Hekryn, Drayd, Kuln, all of them. Each hungry for revenge and glory, each imagining herself bringing home the most spectacular kill and earning a place in the Planetary Governor's mansion of her homeworld. Perhaps even a seat on the Confederation Council itself. "Can you cut through the jamming?" she demanded urgently.

"We're trying, Fleet Captain," Neltryn replied, bending over the shoulder of her communications officer. "The enemy is using some form of quark pulse scrambler wave we've never seen before. Sensors are unaffected, but communications are fried. We're trying to divert power from the main engines to boost the signal, but—"

"Use the robot probes as message pods! Try to get through to at least one of those ships!"

"I'll try, syr, but the enemy swift-strikers are killing our probes as fast as we send them out." Neltryn looked at her, an intensity in her eyes. Her forehead glistened with sweat. She held her voice steady. "They've effectively cut us off from Unit One, syr."

Kaylenn lowered her eyes, her knuckles turning white as she clutched the spear even tighter. "Can we communicate with the other two units?" she asked.

"Barely, syr. It gets harder the closer we get to the enemy fleet."

"Transmit the following message to all ships still in com range: Break the circle. Once transmission is complete, attack the enemy formation. Hit and run pattern. Score as many kills as you can, but stop them from closing that circle!" She silently prayed to her matron goddess that enough of her captains would put loyalty before ambition and follow her lead.

"Yes, Fleet Captain," Neltryn responded, giving a new course heading to her helm officer. Kaylenn followed the course of her ship's attack run. Neltryn had lined it up well. Her gunners concentrated on the drive sections of the enemy ships, aiming for their main thruster pods, where the magnetic shielding was weakest. Four other ships followed her in, but the rest went off on their private hunts, scoring spectacular but valueless kills. The crescent formation held. Kaylenn ground her teeth as the circle began to close.

Five enemy battle cruisers sped in from five different angles, lancing in upon Kaylenn's fleet in a five-pointed star pattern. She recognized the computer I.D. on the attackers, the fast new Zaarin-class destroyers the Vedrans had just deployed. Small, light and swift as Kral's own claws. They were hopelessly out of range, and Neltryn's people still had not found a way through the jamming. Kaylenn stared at the V.R. display in wide-eyed horror as the five advance destroyers swept through what was left of Baltryk's jumbled fleet unit, picking off her ships like flies. The black void of the V.R. vision lit up with computer-generated explosions. The V-shaped formations of the enemy attack groups formed up behind the five lead ships and moved inward toward the center of the circle, preying on her scattered ships at will. Her heart sank. "No," she whispered.

She removed the V.R. helmet and looked at Neltryn. The captain stood stiffly at her station, looking directly at her, as though awaiting orders. Grief was coldly reflected in her eyes. Guilt stabbed at Kaylenn's heart. By every rule she knew, she was beaten. She had only one arrow left to shoot. What did it matter now? She accessed the launch bays and spoke into her headset microphone. "Lieutenant Commander Saaryth."

"Receiving, Fleet Captain," Saaryth's voice replied.

"We're drawing the enemy out for you. Kill them.

Now."

"Received. Execute."

Cold as a computer, by the sound of that voice. They have good fighters, Kaylenn thought, donning the V.R. helmet. *They might be able to do considerable damage. At least our destruction will not go unavenged.* She sighed. She could not deceive herself. This Saaryth seemed capable enough, but without communications, what could she do? Kaylenn watched the computer representation of Saaryth's fighters leaving the *Kalthaar's* launch bays, a swarm of tiny blue triangles. Clearing the ship, the squadron splintered into five precise, diamond-like groups of four. Kaylenn could not believe her eyes. She knew how tricky that kind of precision flying could be, even with radio guidance.

The five groups peeled off, each group attacking one of the five lead ships of the enemy attack formation. Kaylenn's jaw nearly hit the deck when each fighter group, upon reaching its target, broke into four independently targeted fighters. Flying in perfect coordination, they enveloped each of the five enemy leaders and blanketed them with laser fire. Dozens of small orange circles appeared in the computer sim, signifying hits on the five Zaarin-class cruisers. Impossible, but it was happening. Or, was it? She put aside the V.R. helmet and activated the hologram view. One of the beleaguered enemy ships filled the room. Four tiny black metal hawk-like attackers spun round and round the ship's weapons arrays in a sort of pinwheel maneuver, scoring hit after hit. The enemy ship's laser turrets exploded, followed by its particle beam turrets and finally its fuel bays. Geysers of orange fire breached the ship's hull from the inside out. Its hull bloated and exploded in a mass of blinding white-hot gas.

Shaking off her momentary numbness, Kaylenn programmed a sweeping run on the ship's external viewers and put it on holo. The viewer's perspective swung across the star fields, finding the other four Vedran lead ships also under attack by Saaryth's fighters. Bright orange explosions and lancing blue beams of destructive energy filled the black void. "Course zero-five by eight zero one," Kaylenn ordered, overlaying attack grid coordinates on the holo-display of the nearest Vedran lead ship. "Bring all P.B. turrets to bear, and fire at will." Neltryn quickly instructed the gun crews, and the *Kalthaar* made her run. Her beams lashed out and struck the thruster and drive sections of the beleaguered enemy ship.

Saaryth's pilots were in the line of fire, but they stayed on the enemy destroyer and continued firing. Amazed, Kaylenn zoomed in on the holoview and saw the fighters were concentrating their laser fire on the laser batteries and P.B. turrets. They were protecting the *Kalthaar* at the risk of their own lives! One of the fighters was hit by enemy laser fire and spun, damaged into space. Kaylenn expected the pilot to turn her craft toward the *Kalthaar* and attempt an emergency landing. Instead, she turned toward the enemy ship, crashing in a ball of flame against the main gunnery tower, wiping out the bridge section and all that remained of the shield array.

The remaining fighters spun off in a perfectly synchronized maneuver. As the ship dissolved under the *Kalthaar's* barrage, Saaryth's fighters split up and set their headings for the other three targeted ships. That number was quickly reduced to two. Then one. The other destroyers in Kaylenn's battle group had followed her example and launched their fighters as well, Kaylenn realized. The star-shaped maw of the enemy's trap was now a pentagram of five blazing orange infernos hanging in space. The enemy fleet, suddenly stripped of its fleet captain and her squadron commanders, quickly deteriorated into chaos. It was every Vedran captain for herself now.

"Fleet Captain. The enemy jamming is breaking up," Neltryn announced with a beaming smile crossing her face, her finger tapping her radio headphones. "All our captains are calling in, reporting kills. The enemy is scattered and in full retreat, syr!" The crew cheered wildly as the blue arrows signifying their sister ships swarmed across the star fields, hunting and killing the red arrows representing the enemy ships. Flaring white circles appeared as the enemy ships were destroyed one by one, popping like a hail of fireworks. "Shall I give the order to pursue, Fleet Captain?" Neltryn asked, a predatory smile crossing her face.

"Negative," Kaylenn replied. The smile slipped from Neltryn's face. "I don't want to spread the fleet thin or waste precious time or fuel just so a few captains can score points or medals. Our supply ports at Keltrys IV need that fuel and that's our priority. Recall our fighters and deploy a fleet unit to escort that convoy to the Keltrys system."

"Yes, Fleet Captain," Neltryn said in a dry voice, giving the order over the intership com band. Her shoulders heaved. Her breath was rapid. The fire of the hunt was in her blood, and Kaylenn had taken the kill from her. She sensed the disappointment of all her officers. It hung over the bridge like oppressive summer heat. Morale might be bolstered by this victory, she thought, but the moment her leadership came into question, all would be lost. Clasping her mother's spear, she glanced up at the holoview and saw Saaryth's fighter group in tight arrowhead formation, heading back to the *Kalthaar* on a graceful blue-white burn of vented plasma.

Casting her eyes across the entire hologram and studying the computer analysis, she saw all the other Kaltaarist fighters returning to their base ships in similar formations. She shook her head in awe. Such perfect coordination. In a dozen offworld sorties, she had never seen its like, even from the best of Kralite pilots. Her own ships were still only haltingly breaking off their pursuit of the fleeing Vedran destroyers and reluctantly returning to fleet formation. Kaylenn raised the incoming fighter group on her personal com band. "Lieutenant Commander Saaryth?"

"Acknowledging, Fleet Captain."

Kaylenn felt an odd sense of relief at finding Saaryth was still alive. "Well done, Lieutenant Commander. Please extend my congratulations to your entire squadron, and my condolences for your losses. I will certainly recommend you for decoration once we reach Keltrys." It was humbling, talking this way to a Kaltaarist. What would her mother have thought?

"Thank you, Fleet Captain. However, Kaltaarists do not give or accept decorations. We live for each other. Nonetheless, I will extend your sentiments to my people. Saaryth out."

"Insolence!" Neltryn said, having caught the conversation on her own radio link. "Shall I discipline her, Fleet Captain?" Her eyes flashed with anger.

Kaylenn glanced around the bridge, and could see by the tensing muscles, hopeful glances and cruel smiles of her officers that they wanted her to put the Kaltaarists back in their place. Their anger was just as manifest, though repressed, when she answered. "No. Not necessary. They're different, that's all. Let's use that to our advantage. Neltryn, download all computer logs for our report to Fleet Command, and proceed to Keltrys immediately."

Neltryn saluted stiffly and obeyed. Kaylenn

clutched her spear tightly, resolving to watch her back
from now on.

Chapter 3

Timeline: Kalthaar Experiment
Timeline Spatial: The Keltrys system in the galaxy of Kalthaar
Timeline Chronological: The fourth millennium after the age of Kaarth, section point 120799

The officers and crew of the *Kalthaar* and her sister ships celebrated their victory with gusto on the Keltrys IV space station. In the main recreation area, the tables shook as a hundred Kralite femes pounded in applause, red and blue lights flashing wildly across a stage where beautiful young Kaltaarist femes in scant silk garments gyrated to the blaring music. Victory songs and martial salutes to each of dozens of matron goddesses fueled the femes' fervor.

As Kaylenn stood by a viewport, looking down on the blue-green surface of Keltrys IV and on its second moon now peeking over the horizon, she noticed her own name and those of several of her captains had been included in the new ballads. Baltryk and her brave warriors were mentioned as having earned a place in the hunt of the goddesses in the land beyond. No mention of Saaryth or any other Kaltaarist.

The loud music and revelry was a jarring change from the drab, solitary quarters Kaylenn had just visited on the *Kalthaar* and the other ships in her fleet. There had been the usual well-rehearsed speeches and consoling gestures for soldiers mourning the loss of friends, sisters and lovers. Answered, as always, by false courage and brave words forced out through trembling voices, tear ducts struggling to clamp down on the flow over reddened eyes. Warriors did not long mourn for the fallen. That was a sign of weakness.

As always, there were the usual token offers of

financial assistance to friends and lovers left behind, contributions to the temples of matron goddesses, and occasionally the offer of aid to home villages for those few Kralites who maintained contact with their agrarian home clusters after achieving warrior status. The Confederate Council had to make a few such gestures to keep the planetary administrations happy and united behind the war effort. *But here...here celebrated the victors*, she thought with a strange melancholy. *The ones worthy of Kral. Kral who, unlike Kaltaari, loved only the strong and the ruthless.*

Sipping at her drink and scanning the room, she noticed Neltryn and a group of officers drinking at a table near the stage. Thinking this might be a good opportunity to fortify her position, she walked toward them. They all stood and saluted as she approached. "At ease," she said with a smile, setting her glass on the table and pulling up a chair for herself. A look of tension appeared on Neltryn's face.

The other officers politely excused themselves and quickly moved to the other side of the room, leaving Neltryn alone with Kaylenn. Kaylenn took a swallow of her liquor. The message was clear enough. They were giving Kaylenn a choice. The lines had been drawn. Kaylenn sighed and looked at Neltryn who sat quietly, looking at her. One chance to make her case, to win her loyalty? A second swallow brought a buzz to her head. Fair enough, but she would not beg or bargain. "Did you send the report of our victory to Fleet Command?" she asked.

"Yes, Fleet Captain."

"And I assume we'll all be going home to a victor's welcome?" she asked with a smile, raising her glass in toast. Neltryn shrugged, casting her eyes down and rubbing her fingers against her glass. "Is there a problem, Neltryn?"

Neltryn cleared her throat and looked up, her eyes slightly reddened about the edges by liquor. "I had hoped to bring this to your attention at a later time, Fleet Captain. Fleet Command finds our computer logs of the battle to be unacceptable in their present form."

Kaylenn had feared this. She felt a slight chill, but shook it off. "Please explain."

"They think the role of the Kaltaarist pilots should be edited from the logs. They've already deleted all mention of the Kaltaarist squadrons from the official record, and they expect us to modify our logs accordingly, to avoid any discrepancy later."

Kaylenn stared at her subordinate and friend for several seconds. "Have you done so?" she asked calmly.

"No, Fleet Captain. I concluded it was your decision." She looked at Kaylenn with calm, steady eyes. So, there it was. The one and only offer of redemption. If Kaylenn agreed to alter the logs, then she would be re-accepted into the affection of her sister Kralites. On their terms, of course. If she refused, she had best learn to sleep lightly. She would not be the first commanding officer to perish under questionable circumstances in a time of war.

"Fleet Command may have misread certain aspects of the logs, Neltryn," she said in a matter-of-fact tone. "The transmission may have been faulty; residual jamming, ion interference. I suggest you re-transmit the logs in their present form. Just to be sure Fleet Command understands just how valuable the Kaltaarists are to this fleet, and to the Helkan cause. Oh, and please attach a copy of my personal commendation for Lieutenant Commander Saaryth and her people, as well as my commendation for you and your command staff." A clear answer, all the way up the chain. Delivered with a clear offer of reward in exchange for loyalty.

Neltryn's eyes flared a bit, in obvious surprise. Not many fleet captains would dare defy Fleet Command, even after a victory this spectacular. Kaylenn was hoping Neltryn would respect her courage, even if not her judgment. She waited a few seconds for a reply. "I understand, Fleet Captain. I will send the transmission immediately."

As Neltryn started to rise from her chair, Kaylenn gently laid a hand on her arm, trying not to appear desperate, but hoping to play on a mutual attraction she had sensed for some time. "No hurry, Neltryn," she said with a smile. "We are on leave, after all, until we receive our flight orders. I had hoped you and I might take a shuttle down to the surface. There's a lovely little coastal spot on the far tip of the southern continent. A kind of villa overlooking the ocean. I visited there once, a few years back. The setting suns are beautiful against the sea. Flaming orange fading to turquoise and blue at twilight." She gently stroked Neltryn's hands, seeing a clear sign of arousal in her eyes. "At dusk, three moons bright and silver over the waters. The waters are very warm by night there," she whispered to her, leaning across the table.

"Thank you, no, Fleet Captain," Neltryn said, pulling back and taking a large swallow of her liquor. "I have made other arrangements." Kaylenn followed her glance to the other side of the room and saw her officers watching their conversation, apparently with great interest. Neltryn stood up and saluted. "I pray you enjoy the remainder of your stay at Keltrys, Fleet Captain," she said with cold courtesy as she turned and walked over to the other table. Kaylenn sighed in bitter disappointment, finishing off her drink. Neltryn had been her last hope. Now, she was on her own.

Chapter 4

Timeline: Kalthaar Experiment
Timeline Spatial: The Keltrys system in the galaxy of Kalthaar
Timeline Chronological: The fourth millennium after the age of Kaarth, section point 120799

Kaltaarist village songs of joy and gratitude filled the hangar deck as Kaylenn entered unannounced. "Fleet Captain on deck," Saaryth announced as she glanced up and saw her. The circle of Kaltaarist pilots stood up from their seated, cross-legged positions on the floor to greet her.

"As you were," Kaylenn ordered, raising a hand. She looked at their eyes, and could see there had been tears. But only moments ago she had heard laughter.

"May I offer the fleet captain a drink?" Saaryth asked, extending the bottle they had been passing around. Kaylenn recognized the label on the exotically carved glass vessel. Velnyr, a Kaltaarist wine. She had tried it once. An unusual flavor and a deceptively numbing effect. Though alcoholic beverages had almost certainly been a Kralite invention, Kaltaarists had refined the art with their own particular skill. As they had warfare, apparently.

"Thank you, no," she said politely. The smell of Kaltaarist wine on her breath was the last thing she needed right now. "I didn't mean to interrupt your...gathering." She was unsure whether to say 'festivities' or 'services.' Among Kaltaarists there was scarcely a distinction, some said, with life and death changing places like partners in a dance. "I came only to offer my personal commendation on your services and to offer my deepest condolences for the comrades you've lost."

"Thank you, Fleet Captain. Though I have already given your message to the entire squadron, as you instructed."

"I see. Well...if you require any particular memorial services..."

"None, Fleet Captain."

"Very well. If you need to contact your home villages to make arrangements—if any financial assistance to your relations back home are needed—"

"Contingency arrangements have already been made, Fleet Captain. Each village is always provided for by its regional collective." Kaylenn noted a few repressed grimaces of involuntary disgust from the other Kaltaarists. As if the suggestion that special considerations were needed offended them. The very notion of a society in which the individual is left to fend for herself was anathema to them. "As for notifying our home clusters—it seems only proper they be notified through standard channels, as I presume will be the circles of Kralite warriors killed in this war."

"Yes. Of course." Stone wall. Well, since all conventional forms of bribery had proved ineffective, there was only one thing left to offer. Risky, but then there were no safe paths left to choose from. "Lieutenant Commander, I request the pleasure of your company. Would you join me on a shuttle excursion to the surface?" She felt the worried stares all around her, and the hot anger of betrayal when Saaryth replied.

"With pleasure, Fleet Captain." She handed the wine bottle to one of her officers who accepted it with some visible reluctance. "You're in charge until I get back, Ventrie. Keep my bed warm for me," she whispered, leaning forward to kiss the attractive young feme who kissed back.

"Always," Ventrie replied with a smile.

A clear message to both of us, Kaylenn realized. To Ventrie and the rest of the squadron: *Don't worry. My place is still with you.* To Kaylenn: *Don't get your hopes up.*

Saaryth handled the controls as the space shuttle cleared the orbiting station and descended toward Keltrys IV. After clearing her flight plan with station control and the flight center on the planet surface, she swung the shuttle skillfully around the ring-shaped superstructure of the gigantic military space wheel.

There, visible on the station's planetside space dock was the *Kalthaar*. Battered and charred about the edges, but still the pride of the fleet, Kaylenn thought with a smile. As Saaryth did a close fly-by of the docked ship, Kaylenn looked through the viewport and saw the flitting white specs of the space crews moving about with their thruster packs as they worked on the *Kalthaar's* damaged sections.

"I'm told the *Kalthaar* should be battle ready in about four standard days, Fleet Captain." Saaryth's voice held no inflection or emotion.

"Yes, so I've heard. How do you feel about getting back into the fight, Saaryth?" The planet surface, bright green and blue, rose toward them in the viewport.

Saaryth's eyes never left the controls. "I do not relish the thought of losing any more of my sisters, Fleet Captain," she said calmly. "But, as our priestesses teach: If some must be lost on the hunt for the tribe to go on, that is the wisdom of Kaltaari."

There was a note of sadness hidden under her stoicism. And, just a hint of anger. "You must resent my kind for putting you and your sisters in this position, Saaryth."

She sighed, glancing up at the planet's curve now filling the viewport. "Yes. I suppose I do." Her jaw was a bit clenched. Kaylenn hoped letting Saaryth vent her anger in this neutral setting would help gain her trust. But now, it was Kaylenn's turn to open up. "It's a stupid war, I know. The Confederation and our former trading partner, the Vedran Alliance, wasting lives and funds over contested solar systems whose resources don't begin to justify the cost."

"The Galaxy, like the daughter of Kral, belongs to the strong," Saaryth said, reciting the Confederation war slogan, as she raised the shuttle's heat shields and prepped the ship for atmospheric entry.

"More accurately, the next Council term belongs to those ministers who have a successful military campaign to their credit."

"You must be resentful as well, if you believe that," Saaryth said as she switched the ship from nuclear space drive to air-cooled rocket propulsion. The ship trembled and the energy barrier beyond the viewport glowed white hot as the ship dove into the atmosphere.

Kaylenn was at once refreshed and a bit taken aback by Saaryth's honesty. "I suppose, to some extent. The rules of politics and of war are the same as the Hunt of Kral: only one victor allowed. There's no way around that. At least in Kralite society. But a good warrior understands the value of allies. The Council does not." Saaryth remained silent, as though waiting for Kaylenn to say more. *She's not going to make this easy.* To be more direct meant putting her life in Saaryth's hands. Well, she had once already, she reminded herself.

"You've been honest with me, Saaryth, so I'll be honest with you. My government has asked me to suppress the role your people played in this battle, and I've refused." Saaryth looked up suddenly, unable to hide her surprise. "That puts me in a very dangerous position. I don't believe my own crew or officers would assassinate me, even under Fleet Command orders, but I suspect some might be slow to defend me the next time I'm ordered into the line of enemy fire. I have to be certain the same is not true of you and your people."

Saaryth sighed, dropping the mask of composure and suddenly looking very irritated. "Fleet Captain, may I ask what you sought to accomplish by taking such a foolish risk?"

Kaylenn was completely unprepared for that. "I...I want my people to recognize what your people have to offer us. Saaryth, before this mission, I didn't believe a Kaltaarist could be a real soldier. I was typical of my people, but I realize now how wrong we've been. We've allowed a valuable resource to go to waste because of a stupid cultural prejudice. A stigma. If my superiors could just look beyond their stodgy-"

"You are a fool," Saaryth said coldly, looking directly at Kaylenn with stern eyes.

Kaylenn was stunned, but quickly recovered. "You overestimate your value to me, Lieutenant Commander," she barked, her anger surfacing. "Perhaps I could secure my position with my superiors by arranging a convenient accident for you."

"I'll gladly help you to arrange that accident, if it will secure the future of my people," Saaryth snapped back, setting the ship on auto-pilot.

Bright pink and violet cloudscapes raced past the viewport, framing Saaryth's angry, beautiful face. "What are you talking about?" Kaylenn demanded.

"Your superiors are already well aware of what our pilots can do. That's why we're here." Her eyes shifted a bit, as she hesitated. Then she locked eyes with Kaylenn and continued. "Our planning committees have discreetly negotiated with your ministers. We've agreed to help them with their war, and in return they have agreed to divert badly needed resources to some of our worlds which have been left to near starvation since this war began. The only condition is that we do not accept credit for any victory we participate in."

Kaylenn understood. "But you agree to accept the blame for any defeat."

"Of course. We care nothing about that, only about feeding our clusters and helping our people survive this war. And now you interfere with this reckless act of defiance and ask me to put my own people at risk to protect you! Why have you done this to us? What do you hope to gain?" Her eyes flared with anger.

Kaylenn almost smiled. At least now she knew where she stood. "Saaryth, listen to me," she said quietly. "My leaders are shortsighted fools, and the trouble with you Kaltaarists is you have too much faith in sapien love. Don't turn away from me! Listen. The Vedrans have learned the value of training Kaltaarists as soldiers. It's only a matter of time now before they and every sapien empire begins doing the same. Things are going to change for your people, whether you want them to or not. Whether they change for better or worse depends on you and others like you."

Saaryth looked at her with a hesitant curiosity. "What do you mean?"

"Play the game by the Council's rules, and your people will become scapegoats for every disaster Helkos suffers in this war. The few crumbs the politicians toss your way won't help you against the backlash that will follow when this war is over. You think your planets fare poorly now? Just wait. When the next war comes, it will be harder for the Confederation to use your kind as fighters again. But our next enemy won't have that problem, you see?"

Saaryth looked shocked. Almost like a child.

"Our politicians aren't like your planners. They

think only of themselves, not of the problems their successors will inherit."

Saaryth glanced about nervously. "How then does your defiance help us?"

"If enough captains like me and enough squadron commanders like you stand together, they can't keep the truth bottled up. We can build a legend together, Saaryth—you and I!" She felt hot blood racing as she laid a hand on Saaryth's arm. The dark-eyed feme looked a bit frightened, almost as though confronted with a maniac. Kaylenn calmed herself, withdrew her hand and reined in her ambition. "What I mean is that we can help turn public opinion in your people's favor. In Kralite society, military success is the first step toward political power. Imagine your councils having a say in how the Confederation is run!"

For an instant Saaryth's eyes sparkled, then an instant later, darkened with fear. Then they turned away and the cold, defensive calm returned. "No. We want no part of your politics."

"Isolation is a luxury you can no longer afford! You've learned to kill. Now learn to reap the benefits of the kill. As you do on your hunt. As we do on ours."

Saaryth dropped her head back against the headrest of her flight seat. She closed her eyes, the cloud-veiled red sunlight streaming through the viewport painted her face in a wash of blood. "When I was a young girl in my village, our priestess would scold my classmates and me for hoarding food, or not dividing the workload evenly, or fighting over the attentions of a friend. 'The moment you let jealousy or selfishness or greed into your heart, you become like Tryl, the Mother of Evil who stabbed her own sister in the back and sold her soul to the demon Kral so she alone could claim the daughter who brought all suffering into the world.' I never really took any of that seriously. Until now."

"You've come this far," Kaylenn said, feeling genuine sympathy for Saaryth's pain. She had never felt sympathy for weakness before, and feeling it now frightened her a little. She had never imagined that kind of struggle could take place inside so capable a warrior as Saaryth. "You know you can't turn back. You and I need each other."

Saaryth raised her head and glared at her. "And, that's why we're here together?"

"It's not the only reason," Kaylenn said, hiding nothing as she gently ran a hand across Saaryth's face. The other feme's features softened. "Unless you're blind, you saw that the moment we met." Saaryth took her hand in both of hers and kissed it. She stroked Kaylenn's hand softly against her own cheek and looked into her eyes. "I've been honest with you about what I want."

"Power."

"Power I would eagerly use to help those I love. Tell me what you want."

"A better life for my people."

"And, for yourself?"

Sunlight broke through the clouds and washed in a warm orange glow over Saaryth's face. "That, you already know." She smiled, and Kaylenn felt a great warmth passing through her as their fingers interlocked.

Chapter 5

Ralyn's mind rode the currents of time.

Currents taking shape in ocean waves, warm against soft, tingling flesh. The sound of the surf breaking on a sandy beach touched her mind. She felt the warm night breeze touch moist skin glistening in the light of three moons. She felt the gentle caress of strong hands, the warmth of eager lips. The soft yield of one feme's breasts against another's. Two hearts beating swiftly, hot blood racing.

She played time forward, just a bit.

Kaylenn and Saaryth lay together in each other's arms, their bedchamber dark and silent save for the slow, steady rhythm of their breathing and the soft, distant crash of the waves against the shore. Ralyn sent her robots. They shifted into the possible space-time, gliding into the chamber, a spray of tranquilizing mist riding on a warm gust of seabreeze passing through an open bay window. Saaryth stirred and moaned in her sleep as the extractor needle stung her shoulder. She drew in closer to Kaylenn. Ralyn felt a bitter sorrow as the second robot took the sample of Kaylenn's DNA and both machines shifted back out of time. Ralyn had seen what lay ahead on this timeline, and treasured what time these two had left.

Ralyn's mind slipped several weeks forward along the timeline.

A large moon orbiting a gaseous giant planet. A misty moon of swamps and marshes. Battle craft...heavily armored laser tanks gliding along, five feet above the marsh waters, suspended by magnetic forcefields. In Ralyn's mind the immense, black-hulled mobile fortresses resembled swamp-dwelling water insects flitting across the steaming surface of the marsh as they vied with each other for strategic advantage. The gleaming yellow beams of their laser cannon cut through the dense gray mists, gas pockets and huge clumps of swamp vegetation exploding in fire.

One of the floating battle tanks was hit by the lancing beam of a laser, its hull ruptured in flame and black smoke. The tank faltered, hitting the water and turning toward the marshy bank, a wave of brackish water rising in its wake. As the craft struck semi-solid ground, the fuel from its ruptured tanks spilled into the swamp water and ignited.

Chapter 6

Timeline: Kalthaar Experiment
Timeline Spatial: Third moon of the planet Bekryn,
Vedran-held space, in the galaxy of Kalthaar
Timeline Chronological: The fourth millennium after
the age of Kaarth, section point 120825

"Crew, don battle gear and abandon tank!" Kaylenn choked out through the stinking smoke and marsh gas as she sealed her body armor and pulled on her filter mask and helmet. "Fan out! Saaryth, you're with me." She felt the heat of the fire and saw the flickering yellow of the flames as the boarding hatch dropped open, the tank's interior flooding with smoke. She mounted the heavy laser rifle at its place on the armored shoulder of her battle suit, attaching the power pack lead. "Sweep the jungle and run!" she ordered through her helmet radio. "Head north!"

Saaryth and the other five femes in her crew charged out of the burning hovertank and ran toward the dense jungle foliage just beyond the water's edge. The low gravity made coordination difficult. Kaylenn cursed under her breath as she slogged through the thick mud. She trained her laser on the jungle and fired, swinging the beam in a wide arc as she would a scythe. The rest of her people did the same. Seven beams of shimmering yellow light swept through the immense, dark green ferns ahead of them.

Screams came from the jungle, followed by beams of light. Skaal, the soldier to Kaylenn's left had no time to cry out as the enemy's beam neatly severed her head. Kaylenn watched as the armored corpse crumpled slowly into the muck. Kaylenn screamed and fired at the source of the laser beam. "Forward!" she screamed. She kept her eyes on Saaryth, directing her fire to protect her. "Drive in! Kill them!" Trinnyth went down screaming as her legs were cut from beneath her. Even sprawled in the mud, legless, she continued firing her laser into the jungle. Leafy green plants brushed past Kaylenn's filter mask as she bounded into the jungle. There was a thundering explosion behind her, momentarily bathing the jungle in yellow light. She dropped, bits of red-hot shrapnel raining down around her like flaming hail. The smoldering red fragments hissed and sputtered in the reeds and marshy soil. "Saaryth!" she called out.

"Here," Saaryth answered, off to Kaylenn's left somewhere.

She turned and saw an armored figure crouched in the tall reeds, firing into the jungle. Kaylenn swept another tract of brush with her laser. She could see Saaryth's beam sweeping from her left, Trinnyth's on her right, and one other. Patching her helmet radio into the unit com frequency, Kaylenn beamed out a message. "This is Kaylenn. Who else is out there? Over."

"Zelyth, syr."

"Marn, syr." So, the dead one was Kelnyr. Young. Raw, but tough. Kaylenn checked the energy level on her power pack. Half a charge, and they had burned out a wide piece of jungle. All they were doing now was making themselves an easy target for the enemy's heat sensors.

"Cease fire!" Kaylenn ordered. "Fan out, stay in radio contact, and head for the ridge! Once we're clear of the jungle, we'll get a message to one of our hovertanks. Over and out."

Crouching low in the brush, Kaylenn made her way toward Saaryth. She came upon the charred, dismembered body of a Vedran soldier, her molten armor now a smoldering shell around her corpse.

Saaryth crawled from under a damp cluster of ferns. Water streamed in rivulets down the glass plate of her respirator mask. Kaylenn could just make out her lover's strong, dark eyes behind the fog of Saaryth's labored breath. Their hands joined, bulky metal-cased gauntlets frustrating any true contact. Kaylenn desperately wanted to hold her, but the damned suits made that impossible. "Are you all right?" Kaylenn asked urgently.

"I'll live," Saaryth replied, her voice crackling breathlessly through the helmet mike. "And you?"

"I could use a bath," she chuckled. "Come on, we'll rendezvous with the others on the ridge." As they struggled through the mud and dense foliage, working their way up the sloping terrain, Kaylenn's thoughts spun angrily. She focused on the lined, dark-eyed, dour old face of the Fleet Command officer appearing on her private subspace hololink in her quarters. *The Vedran subspace relay on Bekryn's third moon is an easy target*, the withered old hawk had chirped out, with just the hint of a bitter smile crossing her thin, bloodless lips. *The* Kalthaar *alone could do it.* Fleet Command's intelligence reports on this moon's fortifications had plainly been a compound of lies. How many Helkan femes had already died on this mud ball just so Kaylenn's political enemies could be rid of her?

Kaylenn burned with hatred inside her armor, fantasizing about having those witches in Command taken out and flogged before pushing them out a space station airlock and watching them bloat and explode in the vacuum of space. She wondered if Neltryn had been able to get the *Kalthaar* to safety behind the second moon before the enemy's destroyers had found her. The heat of her rage began giving way to a cold, numbing guilt rising in her stomach. She had done this. Her damned ambition had led her to gamble not only her own life, but Neltryn's, her crew, her ship—and, the feme she loved.

Kaylenn and Saaryth emerged from the jungle, Marn and Zelyth joining them atop the mossy green ridge overlooking the lush valley and crooked, swampy coastline. Bekryn dominated the horizon, a bright salmon ball of cloud-streaked brilliance half visible behind the distant gray mountains. The planet filled half the western sky, its two other moons hanging pale white in the dull copper-blue sky. Kaylenn scanned the valley floor and swamplands with the optic visor in her helmet. Her hovertanks were hopelessly scattered, a few distant flitting black specs against the water, yellow laser bursts and fires glowing in the distance. Most were no doubt already fleeing back to their landing craft, the Vedrans in pursuit.

"Open all com channels," Kaylenn barked out over her helmet radio. "Scrambler frequency to all units. Following message: Retreat to carrier ships, launch and pick us up at—" Her sentence was cut short as Zelyth screamed, cut in two by a laser beam. There was a clap of thunder as her laser's power pack exploded in a blinding flash. "Take cover and lay down fire!" Kaylenn ordered, pushing Saaryth to the ground and falling protectively atop her as a second laser volley flashed by, blasting away a piece of the ridge. The towering black hulk of an enemy hovertank rose over the smoking, blasted crest of the ridge, its laser cannon trained on Kaylenn's position.

"Surrender now, or die," a feme's amplified voice boomed out of the hovertank's observation dome. Kaylenn raised her laser to fire, but before she could even aim, a second hovertank rose into view off to her right, just behind Marn. Both hovertanks landed, one at either end of the ridge. Boarding hatches dropped open, and armored femes poured out. Kaylenn found her position surrounded by ten enemy soldiers, their lasers trained on her. "Throw down your weapons, now!" the voice from the first hovertank ordered.

Kaylenn glanced right and saw Marn had already dismounted her laser and was kneeling with her hands in the air. Kaylenn growled in contempt. She looked at Saaryth, lying there beside her, still holding her laser and looking up at her, as though requesting orders. Over the years, Kaylenn had imagined this moment a thousand times over. To die in battle like a Saardra warrior of legend, her spirit joining the honored dead in the assembly of the goddesses, the spirit of Kral looking on. She looked again into Saaryth's brave eyes, sighed and dismounted her laser.

Chapter 7

Timeline: Kalthaar Experiment
Timeline Spatial: Asteroid mining colony in Vedran space, in the galaxy of Kalthaar
Timeline Chronological: The fourth millennium after the age of Kaarth, section point 120836

"Move!" The shock of the guard's stun prod was like a hot knife entering Saaryth's back. The jolt raced through her, and her head swirled, the bright white floodlamps illuminating the mining tunnel spinning wildly around her. When her head stopped pitching, she felt a grainy layer of powdered stone against her cheek, sharp bits of shale pricking her flesh. One of her hands rested on the soft, warm body of the prisoner who had collapsed from exhaustion a few moments before. "Get up," the Vedran guard ordered, prodding Saaryth's ribs with the toe of her boot. "Back to work!"

Saaryth stood, dizzy as blood rushed to her head. She felt something wet trickling down her forehead and touched it. It stung. Her fingers came away smeared with blood and dust. Two other guards took the fallen prisoner by her arms and dragged her through the mine entrance, toward the lift leading to the surface-level domes of the asteroid. The feme's head bobbed feebly as she was dragged away. "What will they do with her?" Saaryth asked.

The guard sneered in contempt. "Spaced," she said coldly. "Unless they want to gut her for spare parts first. We need arms and legs and organs for our soldiers on the front, don't we?" She smiled, and it made Saaryth ill. "What's that look for, you mewling Kaltie? She was a Kralite. What was she to you?"

Saaryth knew she had to handle this very carefully. Perhaps the guard could be reasoned with. "I think I can get her back to work, if you'll let me help her. My people have meditation techniques, and nutritional supplements I think the hydroponics could-"

"Shut up! The camp commander sets procedure. They don't work, they die, and you're close to death right now! Get back to the ore cutter, you Kaltie whore!"

It was like trying to reason with a two-year-old in a large, strong body. Saaryth could not give up, not while there was still a chance to save the other prisoner. "Listen to me...production is important to your people. You need all the workers you can get. I can help—"

The guard brought the butt-end of the stun prod crashing against Saaryth's chin. Stars flashed across darkness as she fell backward into the dust. She dimly heard booted feet crunching against the stone dust, angry voices all around her in the blackness. She felt someone lying upon her, softly. The touch seemed familiar. Kaylenn's breasts against her own. Was she dreaming?

"Stand aside!" the voice of the Vedran guard said angrily as blackness faded to swirling gray. As harsh white light streamed through the gray, framing the guard's stone-hard features and cold eyes, she could see the muzzle of the guard's laser pointed at her. "For the last time, move aside!"

"You'll have to kill us both." Kaylenn's voice, inches beside Saaryth. She tilted her head back painfully, and there was Kaylenn, lying upon her, directly in the path of the guard's fire.

"Don't think I won't!"

"Don't be stupid. You're behind in production as is. Kill me, and you'll have riots to deal with. That'll set you back even farther. I'm the only thing keeping my people in line. Your commander wouldn't take kindly to your killing a ranking officer. Neither would her superiors in your fleet command, would they? They might need to trade me for some of their captured officers, you know."

The guard glanced nervously around at the other guards and the work details they were covering. Three other armed guards joined her, forming a circle around Saaryth and Kaylenn. "I'm responsible. Punish me, if you need to set an example."

"On your feet, both of you," the guard ordered. "We'll let the second-in-command decide this. Move."

Chapter 8

Timeline: Kalthaar Experiment
Timeline Spatial: Asteroid mining colony in Vedran space, in the galaxy of Kalthaar
Timeline Chronological: The fourth millennium after the age of Kaarth, section point 120836

The wounds left by the neural whips stung as Saaryth shifted in the darkness on her sleeping pad. Every inch of her body tingled with lancing pain. Her wrists still ached from the manacles. At times, it felt as though they were still beating her. The air was hot and filled with the smell of a dozen over-worked femes crowded into a small cell. All around her was the sound of raspy breathing from femes curled in fetal positions on thin mats laid on the hard metal floor. She glanced up and in the dim gray light saw the silhouette of a guard's helmet and laser in the corridor beyond the glass port in the steel door.

"What did you think you were trying to do," Kaylenn grumbled irritably from her mat beside Saaryth's. Saaryth turned her head to look at her lover. Saaryth winced at the sight of the festering red welts covering much of Kaylenn's body.

"I'm sorry," she whispered. "I only meant to save the life of one of your people."

"Let me explain something to you: the only way to stay alive in a production camp is to stay up and working. The strong survive, the weak don't. It's as simple as that."

What kind of monsters were these people? "These Vedrans are savages! I think I'm beginning to understand why your people fight them."

Kaylenn almost laughed, then sighed. "Welcome to life among the daughters of Kral, my first one. We

Helkans are no different. Our production camps are just like this one." Saaryth was shocked. She had never believed Kralite society was as evil as the priestesses had luridly painted it to be in their sermons. Until now. *Had Kaylenn done such things?* She looked at the feme beside her, and wondered, in fear.

"How can you do this to each other?" she whispered in anguish. "Don't you feel anything for each other?"

Kaylenn sighed in obvious frustration. "At the moment, what I feel is pain! Leave me alone and let me at least try to sleep." Saaryth turned carefully on her mat and put her fingers against the back of Kaylenn's shaved head, finding the pressure points at her neck and temples. "What are you doing?"

"Relax. Empty your mind of anger. Forget the shadows of the many. See only the light of the one."

"Don't waste your Kaltaarist gibberish on me! I don't believe—"

"Trust me," she whispered in Kaylenn's ear, kissing her softly on her cheek, then on her naked shoulder. "Rest. Let your anger flow from you. You're so tense." She carefully massaged Kaylenn's neural centers, applying the precise pressures, as she had been taught in her adolescence. "Don't fight the pain. Surrender to it. Let it pass through you and away, like the anger. Like everything." She whispered the ritual chant of the cleansing, modulating the tone of her voice to take Kaylenn to the next sensory level. "Forget the shadows," she whispered ever-so-softly, continuing the massage, accessing the next pressure point. "The many are one. The one is many. Choose the one. Remember only the Mother, Kaltaari." Kaylenn moaned deeply as she slipped into the first level of the trance, and entered a dream vision of Kalthaar, the ancient mother world of her race.

Chapter 9

Timeline: Kalthaar Experiment
Timeline Spatial: Asteroid mining colony in Vedran
space, in the galaxy of Kalthaar
Timeline Chronological: The fourth millennium after
the age of Kaarth, section point 120836

Kaylenn sat perched on a narrow stone ledge behind a boulder, high over the rushing rapids of a river. Beside her lay her former lover, her throat slashed, her blood running red into the stream at Kaylenn's feet. The two suns of Kalthaar were setting behind the distant mountains. Kaylenn heard a sound of claws scraping against rocks down below. She carefully drew a wooden arrow from her quiver and placed it against the rough bark string of her wooden longbow.

She peered carefully from her hiding place and saw the monster Kral, the Mother-Destroyer making its way along the river bank in the gathering twilight, coming for her. She drew the bowstring back, aiming at Kral's many glowing green eyes, and let fly the arrow. Kral screamed a horrible scream as the arrow struck its mark. Kaylenn let fly another arrow. Then, another and another, until Kral was dead. Savoring the sweetness of her victory, Kaylenn turned the dead feme beside her face up. The last of the vanishing rays of the suns fell upon her strong, beautiful, dark features. It was Neltryn.

Kaylenn picked up the blood-stained sword with which she had cut Neltryn's throat and carried it with her down the rocky slope to Kral's dead body at the river's edge. Cutting open the dead monster's belly, she extracted her daughter, bloody and crying. Her little face was beautiful in the growing silver starlight washing over the river bank. Kaylenn gently washed the blood from the infant in the river and held her daughter up in the light of the stars. She had won. Her strength and cunning had proven her worthy of Kral Herself. This child—her child—would accomplish great things. This she knew with a fierce certainty. "Your name shall be Laaryn, my daughter. Which means 'power'." Her heart soared with triumph.

Kaylenn trod wearily through hot, oppressive swamps and across burning deserts, her infant daughter in her arms. The child was wrapped in crude swaddling cloth Kaylenn had made from her own tattered clothing. Along her way, she passed the mutilated, decaying corpses of the other eight hunters of the Great Hunt whom she and Kral had killed. One by one, she snatched up their water skins and drank thirstily from them. She spat out the contents of each in disgust. No water. Only blood. Bitter, stale and clotted.

Her own water skin had long since been emptied. Her daughter cried out in hunger and thirst, and she offered the infant her breast milk. Nearly gone now. Her breasts were drained, her nipples raw and infected. She struggled on, her vision blurring, her throat parched. She bundled the rough, handwoven cloth over Laaryn's head, shielding her from the cruel, relentless heat of the two flaming suns, now high overhead. Rubbing her eyes and trying to focus her vision, she scanned the desert wastes. Nothing but bleached white sand under a dark blue sky. Then, she saw *her*.

A feme, about her mother's age, perhaps, with long, sandy-gray hair braided in a strange style. She wore strange saffron-colored robes. She stood there upon the sands, her robes fluttering on the desert winds. Her dark green eyes studied Kaylenn, and the feme shook her head and sighed in a look of maternal sorrow. Kaylenn started desperately toward her, thinking to kill her for the water she must be carrying. But, the strange feme vanished into the wind, like smoke. Kaylenn stopped in her tracks, puzzled. A mirage? Or a goddess come to tell her she was no longer worthy?

She struggled on, her arms aching with the weight of her burden, her legs turning to clay beneath her. Could it end like this? After all her struggles and dreams? "Kral—and all the goddesses—kill me, but spare my daughter!" she cried out to the blazing suns. The hot wind laughed at her, sand scraping against the hot, jagged rocks like the claws of Kral against sapien bones. Only the strong were worthy, she reminded herself with hatred. Just as her strength was completely exhausted, the desert came to an end. She found herself looking upon a gurgling brook at the edge of a jungle outcropping.

Overjoyed, she scrambled into the water. She tasted it. It was pure and clean. Lifting it in her cupped hand, she fed it to her daughter. She let the water trickle from her hand down Laaryn's forehead, cooling the child's fever. She lay in the cooling waters and drank of their sweetness, the cold water stinging her cracked, dried lips. A shadow fell upon her. She looked up and saw a gigantic beast looming over her. A lumbering, six-legged behemoth of orange scales and spines, with six dark eyes on stalks. Its gigantic spined tail swished ponderously back and forth through the vegetation as the creature stood there, passively studying her. Its dull, empty black eyes regarded her as the animal took a huge mouthful of jungle ferns and chewed them slowly.

She saw a large hunting party of tattooed femes

enter the clearing. They wore simple clothing of bark and carried crude wooden spears and stone-headed clubs. One of them noticed Kaylenn and led a handful of her sisters toward her while the rest of her tribe attacked the large, stupid beast grazing nearby. Kaylenn reached for her sword, but she was far too weak to defend herself or Laaryn. "Stay back," she warned, drawing the sword. The feme leading the others struck the sword from her hand with the shaft of her wooden spear.

"Do not be afraid," the feme said kindly, laying down her spear and kneeling before Kaylenn. "We will not harm you. You and the child need food and shelter. Come with us to our village. What Kaltaari gives us this day, you are welcome to share."

Kaylenn looked at her. She was beautiful. Brown skin, dark hair and eyes. Kaylenn wanted her. "What are you called?" she asked.

"Saaryth," the other replied.

Kaylenn lay in the warm, dark safety of a grass hut, Laaryn asleep in her arms. Outside the hut, a fire burned hot and bright, a group of femes clustered around it, sharing story, food and song. Kaylenn's head rested against Saaryth's warm body as the other feme held her, gently massaging her head. "Let your pain pass through you and away," Saaryth whispered, kissing her on the forehead. She slept. Warm, comforting darkness.   A village of femes sleeping, huddled together against night.

Chapter 10

Timeline: Kalthaar Experiment
Timeline Spatial: Asteroid mining colony in Vedran space, in the galaxy of Kalthaar
Timeline Chronological: The fourth millennium after the age of Kaarth, section point 120836

Kaylenn awoke to find herself back in her cell in the Vedran production camp on the asteroid, femes huddled closely around her, asleep in warm darkness. Darkness suddenly comforting, warmth suddenly welcome. Saaryth's hand gently stroked her forehead. She turned, and her lover lay beside her in the dim gray light, her eyes shining, her lips drawn back in a smile. The pain of Kaylenn's wounds was gone. She felt only love washing through her. They kissed, and for that moment, nothing else in the universe mattered.

Chapter 11

Timeline: Kalthaar Experiment
Timeline Spatial: Asteroid mining colony in Vedran space, in the galaxy of Kalthaar
Timeline Chronological: The fourth millennium after the age of Kaarth, section point 120841

Kaylenn seized Marn's arm just as she raised her miner's drill to kill the feme laying at her feet. Kaylenn swung her around and struck her across the face, knocking her down. The other Kralite prisoners gathered round to watch the fight shouted in anger at the interruption. "Idiots!" Kaylenn screamed, kicking dirt in Marn's face as she sat up. "What was it this time? A few crumbs of rations? Sex? Stupid. This is the third fight in two weeks! Haven't enough of us died on this rock already? Can't you see you're just making it easier for the guards? They don't have to watch us if we kill each other!"

Never a fight among the Kaltaarists, she realized with frustration. They shared their rations—and themselves—with each other evenly. That included Saaryth, she knew. The other day, Kaylenn had attacked another Kaltaarist she had seen laying with Saaryth, but Saaryth had stopped her. "You are my first one!" Kaylenn had screamed in helpless rage.

"We do not have 'first ones,'" Saaryth had answered harshly, though with a hint of doubt in her eyes. "One of us may not own another." That still infuriated Kaylenn, but she had to stay focused. There were a lot more Kaltaarists left alive here than Kralites, even though her people had outnumbered Saaryth's to begin with. They could hold out longer in these damned mines. They helped each other. Drew strength from each other.

"We have to work together, *with* the Kaltaarists, if we're to escape."

"Escape?" Marn said with incredulity, a sneer on her face as she stood up, brushing the dirt from her worker's coverall. "Escape to where? There's nothing above this hole but dead rock and vacuum."

"The next ore ship will land here in six days. We can be ready by then. We kill the guards, seize the lift, and take the ship. Simple."

Marn laughed, spitting into the dirt. "Simple? Like our mission to Bekryn?" A few of the others spat or guffawed. "Maybe if Neltryn were here—"

Kaylenn fumed. "Neltryn is dead. *I'm* all you have now. If you want to survive—"

"Neltryn *would* be alive now...*everyone* would be, if you'd stayed on the *Kalthaar* where you belonged, looking out for the crew. But no, you had to take command of the hovertanks to protect your precious Kaltie whore!" Kaylenn stepped in toward Marn, turned sharply and brought the heel of her hand up against Marn's chin, slamming her jaw against her skull and knocking her flat on her back. As she stepped over her, Marn twisted and swept her leg around, knocking Kaylenn's feet out from under her. Kaylenn tumbled into the dirt.

Marn stood over her, raising the miner's drill above her head, the other Kralites cheering. Kaylenn threw a handful of dirt into Marn's eyes and rolled to avoid the drill. As the drill bit dug into the ground behind her, Kaylenn curled and sprang her legs out, landing a kick that sent Marn sprawling backward. Kaylenn pulled the drill from the ground. Marn tried to rise, but Kaylenn kicked her across the face and knocked her flat. The cheering grew louder and louder as Kaylenn raised the drill to strike. She looked into the faces of the others, the Kralites eager for a resolution, the Kaltaarists sad or indifferent. The eyes of one face in the crowd fixed on hers. Saaryth.

Saaryth stepped forward, knelt by Marn and protected her, as Kaylenn had once protected Saaryth. "Enough," Saaryth said, wiping the blood from Marn's mouth.

The Kralites roared in rage and hatred. The Kaltaarists silently looked on. Kaylenn crashed the drill point into a rock to silence her people.

Cooperation is impossible, she realized with grim resignation. She and Saaryth would have to escape alone.

Chapter 12

Timeline: Kalthaar Experiment
Timeline Spatial: Asteroid mining colony in Vedran space, in the galaxy of Kalthaar
Timeline Chronological: The fourth millennium after the age of Kaarth, section point 120883

Kaylenn breathed deeply as she labored in the heat of the mining tunnel, pushing the ore-laden cart along the track leading to the processing furnace. She had to be ready when the moment came. "Speed it up," one of the two guards ordered, as Kaylenn and Saaryth pushed their two loads of raw ore into the furnace chamber.

Kaylenn forced herself to focus her anger. Her skin still crawled at the thought of what she and Saaryth had had to do for that stinking guard commander to get her to assign the two of them to this work detail. Kaylenn had followed Saaryth's lead. It had seemed to come so naturally to Saaryth. The pleasuring, the subservience. Was that all Kaylenn was to her, she allowed herself at last to wonder. Just one more among countless others to come, pleasured for convenience or gain? Even through the blazing heat of the furnace chamber, Kaylenn felt a chill between her shoulders. Was Saaryth even capable of returning her love? And, if not...what possible bond could they have, other than shared survival? *Stay focused,* she reminded herself. *Fear now means death.*

"Drop the load," one of the guards ordered as they neared the entryport to the smelting furnace. The rectangular hatch blazed white-hot, even this far above the radiation shielding. The shaded work goggles offered little protection. Kaylenn winced, her eyes tearing. It was like standing in a wave of fire. Kaylenn's skin blistered in the heat, her arms exposed, only a flimsy work shirt for protection. The two armored guards hung back as she had expected them to. The tall, cylindrical chamber was filled with the deafening grind and clatter of heavy industrial machines above.

From below came the low, ever-present hum of the nuclear reactor. Saaryth seemed near exhaustion as she pushed her cart toward the entry hatch. She gasped for breath, her muscles straining. Her face twisted in anguish, she pushed the cart against the blazing hatch, lifted it and dumped the load. She collapsed to her knees, then dropped, apparently unconscious, to the floor, the cart dropping with a loud clang back onto its track beside her. She lay there motionless on her side, spent by the heat and exertion. One of the guards went to her, swearing loudly. Shouldering her laser, she stooped to pull Saaryth away from the furnace hatch.

Kaylenn forced herself to laugh. "Too hard for you, Kaltie?" she taunted.

"Shut up!" the other guard ordered, glancing in Kaylenn's direction. With a swift, practiced move, Saaryth slipped the sharpened drill bit out of her work boot and plunged it into the guard's throat, severing her artery. The remaining guard turned her eyes from Kaylenn. Kaylenn leaned forward over the ore cart and swung her leg back in a high, sweeping kick, knocking the muzzle of the soldier's laser off-line with Saaryth. Kaylenn dropped behind the cart just as she saw Saaryth raise the dead guard's laser. She heard the familiar crackle and hum of a laser being fired. She then heard the soft, dull flop of the guard's dead body hitting the floor a moment later.

Dressed in the dead guards' uniforms, Kaylenn and Saaryth dragged their lifeless burdens through the mining tunnel to the lift shaft. As they passed the guardpost by the ore cutter, Kaylenn kept her head low, hoping the helmet visor would hide her face. She dragged the dead feme dressed in her work clothes face-down in the dust, the dead guard's wrists in manacles. Saaryth did the same with hers.

The mine guard's attention was on the workers, of course. She gave only a passing glance at Kaylenn and Saaryth. Two more dead prisoners were not her concern. Kaylenn could only pray she would not notice the charred blast hole in her armor, or the traces of blood on the work clothes. She exhaled as they made it to the lift shaft. As the door slid shut and the lift activated, Saaryth slumped back against the elevator wall and gasped, as though she had been holding a deep breath for several minutes. She raised her helmet visor, and her eyes were glazed, sweat beading on her forehead.

Kaylenn had hated using her like that, but it had been the best way. She had known the guards would not suspect a Kaltaarist of such murderous treachery, or a Kralite of collaborating with her. "Don't relax yet," Kaylenn cautioned her. "Remember what's at the top of this shaft."

Saaryth glanced down at the two dead bodies on the floor, and then at her laser. "Kaylenn, are you sure we have to—"

"We've been over this! We don't have time to secure prisoners! In a few minutes, when those guards don't report in, they'll be on to us. If they have time to alert their space patrols before we clear the system and make the hyper-jump, then we're done. You understand?"

"Yes," she said quietly, nodding and closing her eyes. Kaylenn heard the humming of the lift machinery slowing down. She knew they were nearing the surface.

She looked at Saaryth. Saaryth straightened, lowered her visor and readied her laser. Kaylenn nodded to her. The lift doors opened to the guard station. Two guards talking to each other. One was leaning against a steel support beam, holding her laser over her shoulder. The other had set her laser down and was sitting on the edge of a monitor console. Control station: One unarmed feme in a gray uniform sat at a computer terminal. Young. Attractive. Blonde hair pulled straight back in military fashion. She had just been laughing at something one of the guards had said when she noticed Kaylenn and Saaryth stepping out of the lift. At first she just glanced up at them casually, then seemed to pause mid-thought, and looked up again. Her eyes fixed on Kaylenn for a moment, then at the lift behind her. Her pretty, azure-blue eyes snapped wide with fright. Her mouth opened and her hand reached for the intercom on the panel beside her. Kaylenn blasted her pretty face apart with one squeeze on the trigger of the laser. Saaryth fired, killing the guard by the support beam, just as she looked up. Kaylenn killed the other guard, just as she reached for her laser.

Behind the control station were two hatches, one leading to the surface tube shuttle linking the domes, the other leading to the spaceport. They took the latter. The ore ship was there on its landing pad, the work crews loading the processed ore into its holds and prepping the engines for liftoff. An armed feme in an orange uniform turned as Kaylenn and Saaryth entered the port. Kaylenn killed her. Workers ran and Kaylenn blasted them down as they tried to reach the exits. She took little pleasure in it. She felt like a coward, cutting down unarmed civilians as they ran for their lives. One of them looked up from the loading bay and raised her hands in surrender. Just as Kaylenn squeezed the trigger of her laser, she noticed the tattoo markings on the worker's face. As her guts were blown out, splattering against the yellow hull of the ore ship, Kaylenn realized she'd been a Kaltaarist.

Kaylenn looked at Saaryth, but found her lover's attention elsewhere. Saaryth was busy blasting the com systems, security override modules and computer monitors. There would be no way to override the ship's computer from the ground, to notify the patrol fighters, or to I.D. the ship by its call numbers once they'd gone. The bay was a scattered waste of gutted, smoldering machinery and charred bodies when they were done. They had been lucky. The ground crews had just finished prepping the onboard systems. All that was left to do was kill the two pilots, then enter the launch sequence and be off.

As Saaryth fired up the engines, Kaylenn triggered the radio link to the launchbay control. The ceiling of the dome split open in six sections, revealing a black sky filled with star fields, dominated by the one flaring yellow star of this asteroid's distant sun. Only the rippling wave of a magnetic force barrier separated them from open space. Kaylenn accessed the launchbay system to deactivate the field. "Wait!" Saaryth warned her. "We have to depressurize the bay first."

"No time. Fire the engines now." She'd scarcely finished when armed guards swarmed into the launchbay through three access hatches. Saaryth fired the engines just as Kaylenn deactivated the forcefield and opened the bay to vacuum. On the monitor screen, Kaylenn saw the launchbay flood with flaming gas, shrieking into space as the atmosphere blasted straight up through the open dome. A dozen living femes withered to blackened ash before her eyes, their bodies pulled apart in the maelstrom, charred limbs flung like burnt kindling in a whirl-wind.

Kaylenn's teeth rattled painfully as the ship's cabin shook fiercely around her. She struggled with the altitude controls while Saaryth fought to stabilize the ship's ascent through a geyser of compressed oxygen and ignited fuel. The ore ship was spat out of the dome amidst a blast of fire. Kaylenn watched a shower of sapien ashes quickly freeze in the surrounding sub-zero vacuum and fall onto the asteroid's surface, a black crystalline rain.

Saaryth righted the ship and turned it, achieving a low equatorial orbit around the asteroid. As she plotted an escape course, Kaylenn saw the white domed structures and connecting pneumatic shuttle tubes of the Vedran colony rapidly shrinking against the rocky gray, crater-pocked surface of the asteroid. The barren, craggy little splinter of a world fell away as Saaryth switched to nuclear propulsion and the ore ship lifted into open space. Only stars and blackness filled the viewport. "Kral be praised! We did it!" Kaylenn cried in wild jubilation.

"Don't celebrate just yet," Saaryth said with cold intensity, her eyes fixed on the ship's external monitor display. "There's an incoming ship closing on us. Two more coming up fast."

Kaylenn's heart raced in anger. "Maybe we can bluff our way through."

"They're within scanning range of the asteroid. They couldn't have failed to notice our launch, and I'm reading several satellite transmissions coming from the asteroid. If there were automated security monitors inside the launchbay with sat-link upload capability..." The stars rippled across the viewport and the pilot cabin shook wildly. Kaylenn was thrown violently forward, her safety harness cutting into her chest. "Robot bombs," Saaryth announced grimly. "Set for proximity detonation. Those pilots could have killed us just now if they'd wanted to. I think the only reason they didn't was because of the ore we're carrying. Not to mention the ship itself."

A shrill whistle came over the intership com link and Saaryth opened a channel. "Turn that ship around now," a feme's voice boomed through the speaker. "Or, we'll blow it and you out of space."

Kaylenn closed the channel. "Keep going!"

"They'll kill us! They won't allow one of their ships to fall into enemy hands. You know that."

Kaylenn's mind raced desperately. "Outrun them!"

"An ore tanker outrun patrol fighters? We'd be dead long before we could slip into hyperspace!" Her voice sounded resigned. Kaylenn's breath drew short and rapid. She clutched at her laser as Saaryth turned the ship around and laid in a course back to the asteroid.

"Don't," she said simply, glancing at the laser in Kaylenn's hands. "While we live, we are not completely defeated. Death is surrender."

Kaylenn sighed in anguish, laying her weapon aside for the second time. No lover had ever had this much power over her. She was going against everything she had ever been taught. She began to feel she was more Saaryth's prisoner than the Vedrans'.

Chapter 13

Timeline: Kalthaar Experiment
*Timeline Spatial: Asteroid mining colony in Vedran
space, in the galaxy of Kalthaar*
*Timeline Chronological: The fourth millennium after
the age of Kaarth, section point 120883*

Saaryth screamed. The neural shock passing
through her was like an infusion of acid racing through
her veins. The shock passed and she hung, trembling,
cold and covered with sweat. Her breathing was
shallow, her heart pounding. Her arms ached, her
wrists chafing against the metal clamps holding her
spread-eagled against the metal framework of the
neural shock apparatus.

She looked down and there, about ten meters
below her dangling feet was the floor of the cavern. The
camp commander was standing there, flanked by her
guards, and addressing the inmates, assembled as her
audience, armed guards around them. "These two
killed many of my people in their clumsy, stupid escape
attempt." Saaryth looked over, across the stony shelf of
the cavern's roof and saw Kaylenn, hanging as she
was, her anguished blue eyes fixed on hers. "Neither
one has as yet named the instigator of this attempt. If
they consistently refuse, they will eventually die and
two of you will take their places. And two more after
that, until someone confesses. Either Kralites or
Kaltaarists conceived this plan. You will tell me which,
even if I have to go through every prisoner in this
camp!"

Several minutes passed, and no one spoke. In an
angry tone, the commander ordered her guards to
escort the prisoners back to the mines. Once they were
gone, she turned and looked up, swinging her head

between Saaryth and Kaylenn. "You have thirty seconds before the 'treatments' start again," she shouted at them, her eyes cruel and angry. "I'll spare the one who names the other." She smiled, clearly reveling in vengeance. "Be creative. If you both break at once, I'll accept the more convincing account!"

Saaryth understood the Vedran commander's reasoning, twisted as it was. She wanted to keep the Kralite and Kaltaarist prisoners at each other's throats. If she betrayed Kaylenn, or Kaylenn betrayed her, the others would never trust each other. She looked at Kaylenn, who looked back at her. A look recalling that day on the space shuttle at Keltrys IV, so long ago. A plea. A challenge. A declaration. Saaryth rested her head back against the metal framework and closed her eyes.

"You surprise me, Kaylenn," she heard the commander taunting. "I've heard of your mother. A respectable soldier, that one. What would she say to the daughter she risked her life to win from Kral taking a Kaltie harlot as her first one? Is she more important to you than your own Kralite sisters? Tell me this attempt was her idea, Kaylenn, and you can sit out this war in comfort. You, and any of your sisters you choose to favor, can serve me as guards. Let the Kalties do the menial work, eh? That's what they're best at!" She laughed. "Well, that and the occasional one-on-one. But, personally, I prefer the company of my own kind." Saaryth heard the humming of hydraulic machinery, and opened her eyes. The framework holding Kaylenn was being lowered to the cave floor. The commander walked toward it until she stood face to face with Kaylenn. Saaryth listened, but the Vedran spoke too quietly for her to make out the words. She closed her eyes again, and forced herself to see and feel only Kaylenn.

The Vedran is beautiful, Kaylenn thought, despite herself. A hardy, golden complexion. High, strong cheekbones. Dark, cat-like eyes. A strong, sensuous body under the dark green uniform jacket she wore. She brought her face within inches of Kaylenn's. She could smell her breath, feel the warmth of her closeness, and it aroused her, even through the hate.

"Which do you prefer, Kaylenn?" she asked quietly. Kaylenn cringed as the Vedran ran her hand gently down her face and along her throat. She brought her lips to within an inch of Kaylenn's. "I can make this quite pleasant for you," she whispered. "You know you want it. Say it."

"Come," Kaylenn whispered in a trembling voice. The Vedran smiled as she brought her warm lips against Kaylenn's and slipped her tongue inside her mouth. Kaylenn bit down hard, clamping her teeth into the wet softness until she tasted the copper tang of blood. The Vedran shrieked in pain and pulled away. Kaylenn spat blood into her face. The camp commander's face twisted in anguished hatred, and Kaylenn smiled, licking the salty blood from her teeth. The Vedran roared and smashed the back of her fist into Kaylenn's mouth. There was darkness and a flash of starlight. Then pain and a taste of fresh blood.

"Take her back up to her little Kaltie whore," she heard the commander's angry voice from somewhere in swirling gray darkness. She heard a humming of machinery and felt herself being lifted into the air. She prodded at a broken molar with the tip of her tongue and started in pain as she touched a raw nerve. It was nothing beside the pain that followed. The neural shock blasted through her. Her screams drowned out the commander's laughter. She forced herself to see

and feel only Saaryth.
     She felt herself slipping into a dream...

Chapter 14

Timeline: Kalthaar Experiment
Timeline Spatial: Asteroid mining colony in Vedran space, in the galaxy of Kalthaar
Timeline Chronological: The fourth millennium after the age of Kaarth, section point 120883

Saaryth's hand reached for hers as they mounted the back of Kaltaari. The huge creature bucked and swayed as the hunters swarmed about its feet, climbed up its sharp-edged scales and around its sharp, threatening spines. Saaryth held onto a spine just behind the behemoth's small braincase. Hanging on with one hand, she reached down for Kaylenn with the other.

Another hunter beside Kaylenn slashed her hand on the beast's armored scales and fell to the jungle floor. She barely had time to scream before being crushed under the giant's feet. Kaltaari bucked harder as the hunters stuck Her above and below with their stone-tipped spears. Kaylenn held on and reached for Saaryth. Another feme was thrown off, screaming as she fell and was impaled on Kaltaari's tail spines. Kaylenn strained and swung up, seizing Saaryth's hand. It was strong and warm in hers. She pulled her up, and they held each other on the thrashing monster's back.

Kaylenn felt strangely when Saaryth bid her help the other hunters up the living mountain. But she complied. It was alien at first, this new way of hunting. All the hunters struck as one, all their stone-headed clubs flailing upon the armored skull of the beast. The animal roared a weak, mournful wail and toppled, its six legs buckling under its enormous weight. The hunters clung to its scales like fleas to a hound's back as they rode out the fall. Kaylenn, Saaryth and the others cushioned each other's fall with their own bodies. She felt them all protecting her, and each other, as the beast crashed to the ground.

The impact shook her to her bones, but she survived. Bruised only, since the others had been there for her. They had all survived. She looked at Saaryth, and Saaryth smiled warmly at her. It began to feel natural as they all worked together, cutting the beast open, harvesting the meat they had won together. Kaltaari's womb was opened, pink and frothy. There, a multitude of infant sapiens wailed, their tiny hands grasping at the air, the sunlight falling on their little faces. Kaylenn lifted one of them from the clinging mucous of the ruptured natal sac, her stone knife cutting away a twisted multitude of white umbilical veins. Saaryth took another. Side by side, they shared each other's warmth with their shivering daughters. All around them, the tribe sang the songs of thanks and renewal.

Saaryth. She is the rain. Cool and soothing. She comes to all and takes nothing, but nourishes and comforts. The weak and the strong need her equally, and she gives equally to both. I can chase her forever, fight for her with all my strength and cunning, yet possess her no more than would a common root farmer. For who can own the rain?

Kaylenn's head pitched in agony as she found herself back on the steel frame in the cavern. Saaryth hung there before her, head bowed. Still. "Saaryth!" she called out as loudly as she could, though her skull throbbed painfully. "Saaryth!"

"Saaryth!" the old priestess called to her from the burning grass hut, commanding her help in getting the children to safety. Saaryth ran into the billowing wave of dark smoke, choking and half blind. All around her were the screams of her people, and the cruel laughter of the invading daughters of the demon Kral.

A toddler in her arms, Saaryth and a few other adults and adolescents herded a group of children toward the jungle. Huts burned all around them. Their sisters lay dead on the ground like slaughtered animals. Strange femes with brightly painted faces and feathered headdresses screamed and howled like beasts, killing them. Killing other femes! Other sapiens. They carried long knives that gleamed like the sun. The edges of the blades were stained with the blood of Saaryth's people. She felt something burning in her breast that she had never felt before. She saw a strange, angry light in the eyes of these mad butchers, and wanted very much to kill them.

She sent the others on ahead into the jungle with the children. Picking up the spear and club she had used on the hunt, she charged at the demon femes, her anger swallowing her fear. One of the devils charged straight at her, eyes blazing like a predator on the hunt. Saaryth lunged with her spear. The stone tip pierced the invader's gut. She screamed, her face twisted in agony. She swung her strange knife and split the wooden spear shaft in two. The spear tip remained lodged in her stomach. She swung at Saaryth. Saaryth stepped back and the knife slashed across her shoulder. The monster drew her weapon back to strike again. Saaryth struck first with her club, smashing in the side of the feme's head.

She looked down upon the body of the dead feme lying at her feet, blood gushing from her shattered skull. As if in a waking nightmare, Saaryth lifted the long knife by its curiously fashioned hilt, felt it, learned its weight and balance.

Two more of the invaders were setting fire to a hut nearby. Enraged, Saaryth charged at them, screaming in a bestial, toneless fashion as these savages did. It was a release, she found, like fire rising from her gut and raging forth like a storm. She hurled her stone club and hit one of the demons in the leg. The demon screamed in pain and went down. The other one attacked, screaming. Saaryth swung. Her enemy parried. The two long knives met with a spark and a loud ringing sound. Saaryth's hands ached with the impact, but she fought on. Her enemy was quick and tricky as a jungle snake. Her moves were like a dance. But, Saaryth was the storm. Nothing would stand against her. She drove on, ignoring the pain of her own wounds and forcing the demon trickster backward into the flames of the burning hut.

Saaryth thrust the knife through her enemy's heart. She felt a curious sense of restored balance as the dead feme fell into the flames. Saaryth cried out in pain as the feme she had crippled slashed her long knife across Saaryth's leg. Saaryth lopped off her attacker's hand, then kicked her viciously across the face, knocking her on her back. Saaryth raised her long knife and with a joyous cry, plunged it through her enemy's heart. She was amazed at the ease of killing. Cold horror beckoned from some place deep inside her, as she realized how much she enjoyed it.

Saaryth screamed in agony as something stabbed into her leg with a hard impact. She looked down. Protruding from her thigh was a tiny wooden spear, about the length of a feme's forearm, with short feathers at the end of the shaft. Another struck her shoulder and dug in to the bone. Dizzy with pain, she dropped her weapon and sank to her knees, fire, screams and wild howls spinning all around her.

Her eyes swept the burning village. Several of her

sisters had followed her example and imitated the way of the invader. But they could not stand against these strange weapons the enemy used. Short staffs of wood bent into curves by strong, narrow strings. They used them to launch those deadly little spears that flew so fast, their tips shiny and sharp, like the long knives.

The painted, feathered devils surrounded her, their long knives pointed at her. One of them stepped forward and stood over Saaryth. Saaryth looked at her, expecting to see a demon, but saw something else. The feme was beautiful. A strong, terrible beauty that captivated Saaryth like no feme she had ever laid with. Her body was graceful and strong. Her face striking, even under the bright lavender paint. Her eyes were the fierce blue of a summer sky. Her hair was the red of fire. The long knife in her hand dripped with blood. "You fought well," she said with genuine admiration in her voice, and a more basic emotion reflected in her eyes. "What are you called?"

"Saaryth. Who are you?"

"Kaylenn."

Chapter 15

Timeline: Kalthaar Experiment
Timeline Spatial: Asteroid mining colony in Vedran space, in the galaxy of Kalthaar
Timeline Chronological: The fourth millennium after the age of Kaarth, section point 120883

"Kaylenn," Saaryth whispered as her mind swam through an ocean of pain, her senses reeling from the neural shocks as she shifted in and out of reality.

"I'm here," the real Kaylenn called out weakly from the neural rack at the other end of the cavern. "Saaryth... I told them the escape was my idea. Just confirm it, and they'll let you go."

"No," she gasped out, pain lancing through her temples. "No." A warm, soft hand caressed her face. There, before her was a feme she had never seen before, floating in midair, it seemed. Middle-aged, with long sandy-gray hair oddly braided. Large, dark green eyes loving and sorrowful. A single tear ran down her cheek as she touched Saaryth's face. Saaryth shut her eyes and focused. This was not possible. When she opened her eyes again, the feme was gone.

Kaylenn, in her bright silken robes and headdress, adorned with gold and jewels as befit a living goddess, rode tall and proud upon her gilded sedan chair, held aloft upon wooden poles borne on the backs of two trains of her servants. A canopy of jungle fronds adorned with bright feathers and flowers shielded her from the two suns, now directly overhead. Seated beside her, Saaryth found herself swept away by the vision of power and grace her lover conjured in her as if by some dark magic.

As Kaylenn's body pressed gently against hers, she

felt her heart pounding, her blood coursing swift and hot as fire through her veins. "Look at what we've accomplished, my first one," Kaylenn whispered joyously in her ear, sweeping a hand across the gathered armies of Kaltaarist and Kralite warriors, their weapons raised high, their swords glistening golden in the suns. They chanted the names of Kaylenn and Saaryth. "Thanks to you, our two tribes are as one, learning each other's skills and crafts. Your people are the best warriors I have ever seen. Together, you and I will carve out an empire, my goddess. An empire of justice that will bring all the tribes out of the darkness of slavery and war and into the light of our common vision."

Saaryth gazed into Kaylenn's beautiful eyes, burning with her wondrous dreams, and felt their power working through her.

Kaylenn. She is fire. Light. A star beckoning to me across the black void, offering to share her power. Her fire embraces me. We dance in fire. She rises on wings of flame and carries me to the suns. My world and all I know fall away beneath me, yet I do not fear. She gives me the sky and suns, and that is enough.

A hand slapped Kaylenn's face. Gently at first, then harder. Water splashed against her face. She opened her eyes, blowing water out of her nostrils and spitting. Her vision was blurred. She winced and rubbed her eyes. She realized her hands were free. Was she still dreaming? She was lying down. Where had the dream begun? She felt tiny, sharp stones and rough, gravelly earth against her back. She tried to sit up, then sank back down and groaned in pain. Every bone and muscle felt as though it had been pulled loose and stomped on at least once.

As her vision cleared, she found herself staring up

at the stony gray roof of a cavern, about ten meters above her, bright fluorescent lights arranged on the walls. She saw the familiar and horrifying sight of a metal frame of steel rods: the neural shock device. A feme hung from it, dressed only in tattered scraps of her garments. "Saaryth..." she called out weakly.

"Here, love," a voice said beside her. She looked down, and there Saaryth lay at her side, on the cavern floor. Bruised and weary-looking, but alive.

"Saaryth?" With pained effort, Kaylenn rolled over, her body touching Saaryth's. She stroked her hand lightly across her lover's face, and felt the painful bruising about her own wrists, confirming the reality of her current circumstance. "Are you all right?"

"I'll live," she whispered hollowly, reaching over to touch Kaylenn's face. "You?"

"I could use a bath." Saaryth laughed softly. Kaylenn looked up at the feme who had revived her. She wore a prisoner's uniform, yet carried a laser. Her face and clothing were smeared with blood. After a moment, Kaylenn recognized her. *Marn.* Kaylenn glanced about. She was surrounded by armed prisoners. Not a guard in sight. "What happened?" she asked weakly, looking up at Marn.

Instead of answering, Marn glanced up and pointed with her laser at the feme dangling from the metal framework far above. Kaylenn looked at her again, studying the fine body, the long, dark hair. She realized it was the camp commander. Hanging from the opposing metal rack was another feme. "Who—"

"Her second," Marn answered gleefully, a smile on her bloodied face. "The guards are all dead. We tortured those two until they gave up the access codes for the security auto-cams and sat-links. We've taken the domes...most of them, anyway. We'll control this rock within a few hours, and the space patrols don't have a clue; we control all communications. The next ore ship will be here in two days. Getting away won't be difficult."

"How did you..."

"We faked a riot, and...well, we won, that's all."

Kaylenn searched the faces of her liberators. Kralites and Kaltaarists together. Some embracing. "Why?"

Marn shrugged, not meeting her eyes. "You held out," she muttered. "So did she," she said more quietly, gesturing with a toss of her head at Saaryth. "I never thought a Kaltie would... I mean, not for one of us. We had to respect that. So did they," she said, glancing at the Kaltaarists behind her. "And, you were right. We had to fight together to survive. The guards weren't expecting that."

Kaylenn interlocked her fingers with Saaryth's and they looked into each other's eyes. "I love you," she whispered with a smile.

"I love you. My first one." Saaryth said, returning the smile.

Chapter 16

Eons before Marn led the Kralites and the Kaltaarists to freedom at the Vedran prison mine, Ralyn rode the timelines.

"One like fire, all consuming, brief and alone. One like water, all embracing and eternal. They cannot coexist. One must destroy the other. Yet, they embrace. The water freezes. The fire races through it, carving crystalline lattices of silvery webbing, new patterns forming as quickly as the old melt away. A tower of silver crystal forms, the red flames coursing through it. The red light splinters through the ever-changing crystal matrices into an infinity of colors." Ralyn recorded the words into a memory crystal as the timeline played itself out in her mind.

The two feme societies, Helkos and Vedra, fought on for three more years, until their resources were spent. Worlds stood in ruins, and millions of sapiens lay dead on both sides. Ralyn sighed and shook her head, lamenting the senseless waste. She watched as Kaylenn retired from military service and returned to her homeworld, Zeln, taking her mate Saaryth with her. Ralyn glanced down at the memory crystal in her hand. A line of poetry, she thought with bitterness. All she had of her two beloved 'daughters.' They would never know her. She would never embrace them. But they would live in her memory, and in her soul. And in her true daughter. Not even the Nexus could rob her of that.

And, if the Kalthaar experiment succeeded, she dared hope...it might just conceive a race of femes with the potential to master all of time and space. And perhaps, one day liberate the entire sapien race from the tyrannical grip of the Nexus.

Part II - Of Zeln and Trynn

Ralyn's hand joined with that of her seven-year-old daughter, Faln. "Do you feel them passing through my fingers into yours, child?" she whispered. The child looked down and gasped as the surfaces of her mother's fingers glowed golden-green, solid matter shifting to hazy, shimmering light. The young feme tried to pull her hand away. "Don't resist," her mother whispered lovingly into her ear. "It's hard at first, I know. But don't be afraid. I'll help you through it, Faln. Trust me."

"What is it doing?" the child asked in a quavering, fearful voice.

"The microbes live in us, moving from me to you. They move through time as you and I move through air, and carry us with them. Open your mind to them, child. Don't think. Don't be afraid. Just close your eyes and let them lead you." Ralyn felt her daughter's mind take flight along the web of time. She felt cold, shrieking winds against outstretched feathered wings. Warm sunlight against endless fields of brightly colored flowers. Ocean waves closing over her, sunlight dancing through the depths and across the glimmering sides of multicolored fish. Spaceships destroying each other against spinning galactic spirals...

Ralyn gasped as her consciousness shifted back into normal space-time. "Faln...?" Her daughter glowed like a candle flame, with a fierce brightness that softened to a dull, silvery-blue shimmer, and then to a faint greenish haze. Faln exhaled slowly, her eyes closed. "Are you all right? Faln, answer me!"

"I'm fine, mother," she said quietly, opening her blue eyes and smiling softly. The little one looked down at her hands. "It's wonderful. May I go again? Farther, this time?"

Ralyn was shocked. Even at her present age, she couldn't master the time shift with such ease, much less jump effortlessly from line to line. But, then, her genetic matrix had not been constructed from the DNA of four different versions of the race, as Faln's had been. She feared for the child. If she was this powerful already, how could she continue to hide her true potential from the Nexus as she grew older? "Well...yes, Faln, you may go farther, but...be careful. Remember what I've told you about remaining hidden from the other minds out there in the web. Sometimes, if you're not careful, they might catch a glimpse of you; in a dream, perhaps, or in a brief, shared moment, if your feelings are strong enough."

"I'll be careful, mother," the child said grudgingly.

"Alright. Start slowly, and this time, let my thoughts guide you. Ready? Take my hand." Their fingers joined, and Faln shifted again, her skin shining green and gold. "Tell me what you see."

"Sun setting. Orange and gold, over a city. The wind is soft and warm, blowing through a window, raising curtains made of soft silk..."

Chapter 18

Timeline: Kalthaar Experiment
Timeline Spatial: Planet Zeln's Northern Continental Province, in the galaxy of Kalthaar
Timeline Chronological: The fourth millennium after the age of Kaarth, section point 122924

Saaryth stood before the large bay window, watching the sun set over the capital city of Zeln's Northern Continental Province. Its orange light bathed the steel and glass spires of the urban sector across the bay, turning the water and building sides to fire. Air shuttles and flyers weaved about the buildings, coming and going from the rooftop ports. Pneumatic shuttle trams hummed along, commuters on their way home from work. The wind was warm against her face. It lifted the long, silky curtains, and her light silken robes. After four years, this world still seemed alien to her in so many ways. Yet, beautiful. Like the one who had brought her here. She smiled and ran her fingers through her long, luxuriant dark hair as she heard Kaylenn enter from the bedroom.

"Hello, love," Kaylenn said with a slight laugh as she approached her. She pulled Saaryth to her, their breasts touching as she pulled aside their silk robes. "I have so missed you," she whispered in Saaryth's ear, kissing her on the neck. Saaryth's blood burned as she disrobed and coiled her leg around Kaylenn's body. She had ached for this moment for months. Their work had kept them apart for so long. Economic reports, corporate petitions, appeals for funds to the Planetary Governor. All under the cloak of secrecy, of course. Saaryth still partly regretted encouraging Kaylenn's political career. It had brought them to the Governor General's mansion, but the power Saaryth now

"""

commanded from behind the throne had its price.

"Oh, my love," Saaryth moaned, slipping Kaylenn's robe from her strong shoulders and massaging the rippling muscles of her back. As Kaylenn's strong arms caressed her, she forgot all else, all the concerns of statecraft and espionage fading like the sunset. The wind kissed her naked shoulders as Kaylenn's fingers ran through the coils of her hair. Sensing tension in Kaylenn's muscles, she ever-so-gently massaged the critical pressure points at Kaylenn's neck and temples, until she felt the tension flow from her body. Kaylenn exhaled deeply. "Always tense, my brave Captain," Saaryth said with a giggle, kissing her on the lips. "My brave, beautiful Kaylenn." As they kissed, Saaryth let Kaylenn's warmth flow through her, reaching every neglected recess of her being. Saaryth pressed her lips to Kaylenn's, her fingers running through her long red hair.

"I've so long wanted to hold you, goddess," Kaylenn whispered, kissing Saaryth's breasts. "You are my strength." Saaryth took Kaylenn's face in her hands, pulling her mouth to her own. Their tongues joined. This moment was theirs. Such moments were few and expensive. Saaryth savored them. No guilt or regret. Only love.

Saaryth laughed as Kaylenn lifted her off the softly carpeted floor and onto the divan. Kaylenn's hand reached between her legs as their lips met. Saaryth scarcely noticed the sound of something heavy thumping against the carpeting and clattering against a table leg. She laughed, thinking they might have knocked over a lamp in their eagerness. The sweet pain of Kaylenn finding her way inside worked its way through her. As she threw her head back, her nails reflexively digging into Kaylenn's back, she chanced to glance back and saw the lamp still standing in its usual place beside the divan.

As Kaylenn came down upon her, pressing her back against the cushions, Saaryth twisted her head back and glimpsed something on the floor, beside the table. She could see only a bit of it, the rest hidden by the armrest of the divan. She tried to draw herself up and brace her back against the arm rest so she could look down and see what it was. But Kaylenn was on fire and would not be denied. Saaryth fought to sit up, Kaylenn pressed down.

Something stabbed at the back of Saaryth's mind. There was something wrong. She had to get up. "Let me go," she moaned, fighting her own arousal, her muscles straining against Kaylenn's. She felt Kaylenn's teeth biting into the soft flesh of her neck, and desperately wanted to surrender, but something in her told her she had to get up. "Let me go," she growled, her finger-nails digging into Kaylenn's face.

She levered her well-muscled forearm across Kaylenn's neck and pushed, her shoulders straining. "I said, let me go!" she screamed, landing a punch across Kaylenn's jaw. She pushed with her leg, and Kaylenn pulled back. Saaryth turned her head and looked down at the floor, and there the thing lay. Egg-shaped, about the length of her hand, black metal casing with silver studs and flashing red lights.

Saaryth did not think; she did not have to, her battle training guided her, like a spirit taking possession of her body, firing her nerves and activating her reflexes, launching her off the divan. She rolled across the floor and snatched up the object with one fluid motion. When the war ended four years ago, she had hoped the demons she had had to call upon in battle would be exorcised. She had lamented the fact that they insisted on lingering. Until now. She sprinted across the room. The metal egg was heavy. She drew it back as she reached the bay window.

"Saaryth...," Kaylenn called out from somewhere behind her.

"Get down!" Saaryth screamed as she hurled the object out the window and over the balcony beyond. She heard it clang noisily as it collided with the metal railing. It just barely cleared the hand rail and spun end-over-end as it dropped from the balcony. Saaryth turned from the window, her eyes caught a blurred movement. Kaylenn leapt upon her, knocking her away from the window and throwing her to the floor. Kaylenn fell protectively upon her as the building shook with a roar of thunder and the room was momentarily bathed in a wash of bright orange light. It reminded Saaryth of the sunset.

Chapter 19

Timeline: Kalthaar Experiment
Timeline Spatial: Planet Zeln's Northern Continental
Province, in the galaxy of Kalthaar
Timeline Chronological: The fourth millennium after
the age of Kaarth, section point 122924

Hundreds of pairs of booted feet clomped down ringing flights of metal stairs. Guard commanders barked orders and deployed their troops. Kaylenn stood beside Saaryth at the heart of the underground bunker, her hand still reflexively clutching her lover's, their fingers tightly interlocked. Kolis, Kaylenn's chief of security, ran in, breathless, and stood at attention. "Perimeter secured, syr," she reported with a crisp salute. She stared straight ahead, her dark green eyes looking past Kaylenn's, her wide forehead glistening with sweat.

"How was it done?" Kaylenn demanded, releasing Saaryth's hand and stepping to within a few inches of the tall, powerfully muscled Kolis.

"The bomb was launched from a flyer, syr," she said with the hint of a nervous twitch in her eye.

"Distance?"

"The flyer was within...two meters of the balcony, syr." Kolis swallowed.

"Two meters?" Kaylenn growled through clenched teeth. "How could you let them get that close? Where were your air patrols? Why didn't the security net trigger the magna barrier?" Kaylenn's voice escalated in volume until the last question was a roar.

"They had clearance, syr," Kolis said in a voice beginning to show a trace of fear. "Apparently, they hacked into the security net and downloaded a clearance code. The flyer itself was disguised as one of our patrol fighters. They transmitted the proper recog protocols," she said defensively. "We were notified by traffic control that there was a discrepancy in the flight schedule, but—"

"But not in time to intercept an attempt on my life! If not for Saaryth, your incompetence would have killed us both." Kaylenn took a breath and stared pure menace into her chief of security. "Or am I being too generous in ruling out complicity, Kolis?" Kaylenn's voice was between a whisper and a growl, and would have been very intimate had her words not carried such danger.

The large feme's eyes flashed with anger for a moment, then returned to their icy stare. "I accept full responsibility for this breach of security, Governor General, and offer no excuse. But, any accusations of treason should be made through official channels, and in the context of full court-martial proceedings."

Kaylenn studied the other feme's stocky features, and nodded. She was satisfied Kolis was not involved. *Strong, fiercely loyal, not terribly imaginative, that one. Recruited straight from the factories into guard service. Good soldier, but lacking the ambition or intelligence for advancement. The perfect security officer.* "Do you have them?"

"One, syr. The other was killed resisting arrest. There was an exchange of fire."

"Identification?"

"The survivor's name is Zelkys, formerly a worker from Production Zone Zed-4, along our southern border."

"Formerly?" Saaryth asked. Kaylenn glanced back at her over her shoulder, grinding her teeth. *When would she learn the need for discretion?* She turned back to Kolis. The security chief was scowling in Saaryth's direction, as though angered at the interruption.

"Explain, Kolis," Kaylenn ordered.

"Zed-4 is owned by the Transtar Production Combine, syr. It was an autonomous agricultural project before Transtar acquired it in the planetary land auctions. Some of the agro workers were retrained for the chemical refineries Transtar built over the farmlands. Others hired out as mine workers in other zones. There's been some minor insurrection among the unemployed and displaced in Zed-4. Sabotage of refinery equipment, sporadic bombings and attacks on Transtar personnel. The local security team is handling it."

"Not well enough, clearly," Kaylenn said accusingly.

"Syr, the Zed-4 insurgents are nowhere near sophisticated enough to accomplish something like this without help. My guess is they're just being used by radical elements of the political opposition. Or possibly one of the anti-Kaltaarist groups opposed to the new trade contract with Trynn."

"I want facts, Kolis, not idle speculation! Has this Zelkys named anyone?"

"Not yet, syr. She is still in a military hospital, being treated for wounds sustained during her capture. She is expected to survive. Assuming she does, we will begin interrogating her as soon as possible. Though, frankly, I doubt we'll get anything useful out of her. Whoever is behind this is too smart to have given her much information."

Kaylenn sighed in frustration. "Don't waste time, then. Give her one chance to cooperate. If she refuses, or doesn't know anything...then, make an example of her. Publicly. I don't want to appear shaken by this. Now go." As Kolis saluted and turned to go, Kaylenn felt a hand on her arm. She turned as Saaryth stepped up beside her.

"Stop her," Saaryth whispered in her ear. Kaylenn stared at her with puzzlement. "Please," she whispered with urgency.

"Kolis, hold!" she called out to the security officer just as she was about to mount the stairs. Kolis paused and looked back at her. "What is it?" Kaylenn whispered to Saaryth in irritation.

"I need to speak to you," Saaryth replied. "In private."

Kaylenn fumed in silent anger and clenched her fists. Saaryth's eyes pleaded with her. Kaylenn rolled her eyes in exasperation, then sighed and relented. "Kolis...remain here for the time being. I want to...review the Zed-4 situation before we proceed. Arrange to send all relevant data on Zed-4 to my quarters here in the bunker. And while you're at it, send along any pertinent information on other suspects—opposition or otherwise, that you see fit."

Kolis looked puzzled for a moment, then snapped to attention and saluted. "As you wish, Governor General."

"What in the Black Void did you think you were doing?" Kaylenn screamed, stomping through her quarters and hastily pouring herself a glass of her favorite Kralite liquor, spilling some in her carelessness. "My life is threatened within the Governor General's mansion, which makes me look foolish enough in itself!" She took a large swallow of liquor. "Public image is enough of a problem. The last thing I need is to appear weak in the presence of my own staff!"

Saaryth hated seeing her like this. She realized she was becoming a political liability to Kaylenn, possibly even a danger to her, and it hurt. Apart from simple compassion, why had she interfered? Was it Kaylenn she was afraid of losing, if the execution of her would-be killer was carried out, or herself? "I'm sorry. I didn't have time for anything else. I didn't mean to—"

"Why should you care what happens to her?" Kaylenn snapped. "She tried to kill both of us, for Kral's sake! You've killed enemies in war."

"I had no choice. You do."

"This is war! I have to prove I can protect myself or my enemies become bolder and my administration is finished! And with it the trade contract that feeds your people."

"You have helped my people greatly, and for that you have my deepest gratitude, my love. But what of your own people?"

Kaylenn finished off her drink and started to pour herself another. "We've had this conversation more times than I care to remember," she muttered angrily, taking a swallow. "Transtar won the auctions, so the land is theirs. End of story. I don't like it, but that's the situation we're stuck with."

"The few enrich themselves at the expense of the many. Even after four years here, it seems as insane to me as ever." Saaryth's voice was soft but strong as steel.

Kaylenn sighed deeply, bowed her head and set down her glass. "That's why my people rule and yours struggle for survival."

"Mine don't kill each other." Kaylenn looked up at her, indignation in her eyes first, then fear, as though she were looking at her across a widening gulf. "Love..." Saaryth walked toward her. "What I did, I did out of concern for you. Your list of enemies grows longer every day. They strike at you, you strike back. Against some of them, fear is an effective weapon, I admit. But these workers in Zed-4 sound desperate.

What if they have too little to lose for you to frighten them into submission?"

"They have their lives to lose! They care about that, don't they?"

Kaylenn's blue eyes flashed with a killing rage, and it frightened Saaryth. She laid a comforting hand across Kaylenn's face, and that seemed to calm her. "What will you do if they don't submit?" she asked quietly. "Kill them all?" Her stomach began to turn even at the thought. "What then? If the people believe they must fight you for their survival, you'll have more enemies to deal with. Not just one rebel sector next time, but perhaps three or four. This is your home, Kaylenn! Your people. You're entering a fight you can't win. You must at least try to reconcile; to find common ground with these people."

Kaylenn fumed, turning away from Saaryth and pacing. "And how am I to do that?"

"Go to Zed-4. Assess the situation there for yourself. Let the workers there see you support them and that it is in their best interest to work *with* you in finding solutions to their problems."

Kaylenn turned and stared at her with mouth agape. "I'm to submit to intimidation?"

"Not all the workers in Zed-4 are responsible."

"Not yet. Examples-"

"Must be set, I know. But what about examples of cooperation?"

"My people don't think like yours! They don't react to kindness with cooperation, but with predation. Didn't the war teach you anything?" "Yes. It taught me that my people make better soldiers than yours. Since then, I've noticed we make better politicians, too. And perhaps better negotiators, if given the chance." Kaylenn looked angry. Then frustrated, clenching and unclenching her fists. For an instant, Saaryth thought she would strike at her. But Kaylenn held herself in check. She turned away, trembling in anger, and poured another drink. Saaryth cursed herself under her breath. Kralite curses were becoming second nature to her, she realized. As was the Kralite quickness to anger. She had gone too far, and she had hurt her.

"I'm sorry. I spoke without thinking. But, Kaylenn...you must make allies if you...if we are to survive. Your enemies court the favor of the workers. You must do the same. They see you as an enemy because your rivals describe you that way. They strike at their enemy, just as you would in their place. Show them that your power can serve their ends if they serve yours."

Kaylenn turned and looked at her, a trace of moisture in her eyes. "Where do you suggest I begin?"

"With the one who tried to kill you."

Timeline: Kalthaar Experiment
Timeline Spatial: Planet Zeln's Northern Continental
Province, in the galaxy of Kalthaar
Timeline Chronological: The fourth millennium after
the age of Kaarth, section point 122924

A few hours later Kaylenn looked down at her would-be assassin. Her arm and face were bandaged. Her wounds were not nearly severe enough to satisfy Kaylenn's simmering wrath.

"Your name is Zelkys?"

"What of it?" the swarthy-faced young feme mocked from her hospital bed.

"Shall I teach this dog respect, syr?" Kolis asked, reaching for the neural prod on her belt. A Kaltaarist medic standing by looked frightened.

"Not yet," Kaylenn said, remembering the feel of one of those shock prods against her own flesh in a prison compound years ago. "I'll speak to her alone. Leave us." As Kolis turned to go, the medic stared curiously at Saaryth, still standing at Kaylenn's side. "I said, leave us," Kaylenn snapped. The medic bowed respectfully and left. Kaylenn looked at the feme who had fired a bomb at her through a window. A bomb that would have killed Saaryth even as she lay in her arms. The young laborer looked up at her with dark, hateful eyes. Mocking her with contempt. Kaylenn desperately wanted to kill her. "You attempted to kill me." Zelkys did not deny it, but lifted her chin. "A bomb through a window." Pause. No reaction. "A coward's act," she said with disgust. "The pathetic act of a criminal, not a warrior."

Zelkys sneered at her. "That should be expected, your excellency," she said sarcastically. "I'm not a great war hero like yourself, just a laborer. Expendable fodder for the factories. Still, give my sisters and me lasers like you give the Combine, and we'll fight for our land. We'll kill, like you mighty warriors! Just give us the chance-" She winced in pain, putting a hand to her bandaged head. Saaryth bent over her, placing her hands against her neck, as she had once done for Kaylenn in the prison cell. "What are you doing? Get this Kaltaarist filth away from me!"

"Don't fight the pain," Saaryth whispered, almost too softly for Kaylenn to hear, as she massaged the crucial pressure points. "Surrender to it. Let it pass through you and away, like the anger. Like everything. Forget the shadows. Remember the light. The many are one. The one is many. Choose the one. Remember only the Mother, Kaltaari."

Zelkys moaned in relief, the tension draining out of her face as her head sank back into her pillow, an expression of peace settling across her brow. Kaylenn could not suppress a twinge of jealousy. Saaryth reached beneath her robes and produced a small oval disc which she placed gently against Zelkys's jugular vein. "Don't worry," she whispered as she applied pressure against the disc with her thumb, breaking the surface and letting the liquid contents diffuse through Zelkys's skin. "It's only a neural inhibitor. It will help you deal with the pain for a while."

"Where'd you get it?" Zelkys asked dreamily, looking up at her with calm eyes.

"It's Kaltaarist," Saaryth answered quietly. "From Trynn. Technically, it's illegal here on Zeln, but don't worry. No one will know."

"You...you're her first one," she muttered, glancing from Saaryth to Kaylenn.

"Yes, I am."

"You were there when I tried...to kill her. Why are

you here now?"

"I've helped ease your pain," Saaryth said in a calm, even voice. "Now repay me by telling me why you tried to kill us. What injury have we committed against you?"

"The Combine took our lands. The government sold them all we had. Now our farms are gone. We go hungry. The refineries poison what land and water we have left. Our people are dying."

"And you thought killing the Governor General would improve your situation?"

"The Opposition feme said her party would make things better, like they used to be. She said Kaylenn is a traitor to her people. That she ruins our lands to feed your people on Trynn. That she gives our work and holdings to you."

"That's not true," Saaryth said gently. "When the land auctions were being voted on, Kaylenn was still learning to hunt Kralines. And you, I suspect, were in the womb of one. Kaylenn inherited the present situation when she came to office, and she has been no friend to the Combines. They resent her trade policies, toward Trynn because Kaltaarist trade weakens their control over sectors like yours. As for the Opposition—they would like nothing better than to sell off what remains of your lands in order to enlarge their own power. Only Kaylenn stands in their way. Her enemies are your enemies. If you work with her, we could arrange an alliance which would secure her position here in the Northern Province, and improve conditions in your sector."

Zelkys sighed and closed her eyes. "What do you want from me?"

"Tell your people Kaylenn wishes to negotiate, on condition that they renounce violence and sever all ties with the Opposition. Kaylenn will make a public appearance in Zed-4, as a gesture of good will. Ask your leaders to meet with her to discuss terms."

Kaylenn was shocked. She took Saaryth by the hand and pulled her gently but firmly away from the bed. "I'm to let her go?" she whispered to Saaryth. "Use her as a messenger?"

"What better way to gain their confidence? Let me speak with her further. Trust me." She kissed Kaylenn lightly on the cheek. With hesitation, Kaylenn released Saaryth's hand.

Saaryth returned to Zelkys's bedside. "As you see, Kaylenn has some hesitation about trusting you. I'm sure you understand why. I will not lie to you. You will be prosecuted for what you have done, under the laws and traditions of your own people. We make no promises of amnesty. The circumstances of your actions will be considered in deciding your fate, of course. But if, as you claim, you act in the best interest of your sisters, then you will carry this message to them, and let them make the decision."

Zelkys stared at Saaryth first, in what looked like puzzlement. Then at Kaylenn in obvious distrust. "Is what she said true?"

"Always," Kaylenn replied.

Zelkys paused a moment. "All right," she said finally. "I will carry your message."

Saaryth looked at Kaylenn, as though awaiting her decision. Kaylenn looked into her lover's eyes. She remembered the firefight on Bekryn-III. The aborted escape from the Vedran asteroid base. Each time, Saaryth's indefinable power over her had overwhelmed both Kaylenn's instinct and training. *And is the only reason I am still alive.* She sighed. "Agreed."

Chapter 21

Timeline: Kalthaar Experiment
Timeline Spatial: Production Zone Zed-4, Planet Zeln's Northern Continental Province, in the galaxy of Kalthaar
Timeline Chronological: The fourth millennium after tho age of Kaarth, section point 122925

Kaylenn looked down from the air shuttle over the wasteland that had once been Zed-4. The ugly, gray-steel constructs of chemical refineries stretched across smoldering gray fields of filthy slag. Rivers which had once fed fertile land ran dark and polluted across plains of dead, gray earth. "This is the sector I saw in the holovids?" she asked in disbelief.

"Yes," Zelkys said, seated beside her. "What's left of it, since the auctions."

"But...the agricultural production reports..."

"Falsified," Saaryth said.

"My own inspector general?" Kaylenn's outburst drew the uncomfortable attention of her entourage.

"The land auctions brought in revenue. With revenue comes bribery." She leaned close to Kaylenn's ear. "You see, love, I have been paying attention these past four years." There was both humor and bitterness in her tone.

"It's unbelievable," Kaylenn said as the shuttle passed over a smoking black lake of toxic waste. "Our offworld agro contracts can't survive something like this. Zeln has an obligation to the rest of the Helkos Confederation. There are worlds out there starving since the war, and dependent on our produce! Once the Confederation inspectors get wind of this, there'll be Kral to pay." As the airship sailed on, Kaylenn was awestruck by what she saw next. Forcefield generators, heavy-duty laser turrets and hovertanks formed a line stretching across the ashen plane, surrounding the refineries. "That's quite a defensive perimeter for handling a 'minor insurrection.'"

"We gave them reason," Zelkys said with a touch of gloating malice in her voice. "Look there, to the left, just outside the perimeter."

Kaylenn looked and saw the remains of a large building which looked as though it had been blown apart from the inside out. A gutted shell of shattered concrete and half-melted girders filled with tons of charred scrap. "That was one of their key processing plants," Zelkys announced proudly. "Zaard told us to wait until they'd gotten it up to one hundred percent productivity before we sabotaged the generator." She giggled like an adolescent tasting liquor for the first time. "Zaard had us launch raids against other plants, so they'd post lots of troops here, to protect this one. The bomb was already in place, of course. Boom!" She swept her one good hand up, playfully illustrating the explosion. "Lots of troops, lots of Combine money lost. It worked just like Zaard said it would."

"Smart," Kaylenn remarked with grudging admiration, thinking she would like to have this Zaard as an ally. Saaryth only sighed deeply. Kaylenn looked at her and recognized the cold, unfeeling mask her lover had forged to protect herself during the war. She realized, with some guilt and much sorrow that, save for lovemaking, the face hidden beneath that mask was almost never seen anymore. Did it even still exist?

"When will I have the honor of meeting Zaard?" Kaylenn asked.

Zelkys wrinkled her bandaged face in disbelief. "No outsider sees Zaard!"

Kaylenn was offended. *The impudence!* "Is that any way to start an alliance?" she snapped.

"You promised us a public statement," Zelkys shot back. "Fulfill that promise for the whole of Zeln to hear, and Zaard will send one of her lieutenants to meet with you. She has said this."

Kaylenn smiled. This rebel leader Zaard was shrewd as well as bold. Always give the appearance of being in control when introducing yourself to a potential ally. Or potential enemy, for that matter. *Fine.* It was a game two could play. She wanted a gesture of support? Kaylenn would give her one, and display her own power in the process. "Kolis," she said, speaking into the cabin intercom. "Step in here. I need you."

The door to the pilot section slid open and Kolis stepped through. "At your command, Governor General."

"I want you to bring up both your supporting battle flyers at full combat readiness. Order troops flown in from the capital. Say, twenty thousand or so. And I want at least two bomber squadrons fueled and ready to enter this sector on my command."

Kolis raised one of her thick eyebrows. "Might I know the reason, syr?"

Kaylenn clenched her jaw instead of reprimanding Kolis. If Kolis noticed, she made no indication. "Once you've made all the preparations, contact the commander of that security force below and inform her you're assuming direct command of her forces on the authority of the Governor General. Your first act as commander of this sector will be to shut down the Transtar Combine chemical refineries and arrest all Combine personnel on my authority.

"Close your mouth, Kolis, I'm not done yet. Effective immediately, I am officially nationalizing this production sector and all Transtar Combine property contained therein. All production in Zed-4 will henceforth be under the direct supervision of myself and whatever production managers I choose to appoint. You will announce this publicly upon taking command. I'll contact my staff in the capital and have the necessary documentation drawn up. And, Kolis...at the first sign of military resistance, you are authorized, *and expected*, to employ all force necessary to suppress it. Carry out this directive effectively, and I will be in a position to reward you far more generously than the Transtar Combine ever could. Any questions?"

The large feme hesitated only a moment, before she snapped rigidly to attention. "None, syr."

"Dismissed."

Kolis saluted, turned on her heel and strode out. Kaylenn turned to Zelkys and found her with mouth agape and eyes wide. "Now, do I get an audience with Zaard?"

Zelkys took only a moment to recover. "May I use your com system?"

"At your convenience," Kaylenn said with a smile, gesturing at the communications console at the rear of the cabin. As Zelkys rose and stepped over to the console, Saaryth sat down beside Kaylenn on the padded seat beside the window, taking her hand.

"Well done, love," she whispered, kissing her lightly on the cheek.

"I've been paying attention, too," Kaylenn said, stroking her finger playfully across Saaryth's chin.

Chapter 22

Timeline: Kalthaar Experiment
Timeline Spatial: Planet Helkos, in the galaxy of Kalthaar
Timeline Chronological: The fourth millennium after the age of Kaarth, section point 122925

"But, Prime Minister, this is nothing less than criminal rebellion!" Kelnaath, the Planetary Governor of Zeln barked through the holographic projection beamed into the office of the Prime Minister of the Helkos Confederation. "I personally authorized the Zeln land auctions, and the Confederation Council approved my decision. What Kaylenn has done is in direct defiance of my authority and yours!"

Prime Minister Grath sighed wearily, clasping her hands on her desk and looking up at the projection before her. Kelnaath was a relatively handsome feme; dark skin and large, dark eyes. Curly strands of long, black hair draped over one shoulder. Apparently a competent administrator. *Rather a dark, murky military career, though,* Grath noticed as she glanced down at the printout of Kelnaath's service record spread out on the desk in front of her. Covert stuff. Infiltration, sabotage and assassination. An operative of Division 12, a clandestine unit jokingly referred to as the Dark Sisterhood of Taarex. She had risen quickly through their ranks, apparently displaying a natural talent for that type of kill. She had led several successful missions behind the Vedran lines. Widely reputed as a butcher, but an efficient one. The daughter of a strong gathering; never participated in a hunt herself, though. Rose to power through ruthless cunning in the corporate castes, and through the convenient disappearances of several corporate rivals.

"Kelnaath," she began in a level voice, "if you can't control your own provincial governors, don't expect Helkan troops to come to your rescue. As you very well know, or should, the Confederation Charter expressly forbids military intervention in the internal politics of a member planet. Except in cases of unlawful secession or offworld invasion."

"Or collusion," Kelnaath amended. "Kaylenn is being influenced by that Kaltaarist witch, Saaryth. Her true loyalty is to Trynn, not Zeln. She has demonstrated this time and again."

Grath sighed in disgust. "Trynn is a subject world of the Helkos Confederation. What dealings Kaylenn has with them is of no concern to this office. Nor her taste in sex partners. Your political rivalries with Kaylenn are your own affair, Kelnaath. Deal with her."

Kelnaath's face twisted in anger and frustration. "I thought we had an understanding," she said in a trembling voice.

"I hope we still do. Let's see if you understand this." She pressed a button beside the onyx statuette of her matron goddess on her desk, and the hologram vanished. Grateful to be rid of that irritant, she stood up from her desk and walked over to her Traalk creeper. The large, blue-leafed plant was doing well, its long tendrils beginning to sprout soft, lavender blossoms. Her Chief of State, Raast, sighed behind her. "Something you wish to share, Raast?" she muttered, spraying a bit of water onto the plant's leaves.

"Kelnaath is right about Kaylenn," the stiff-faced feme said in a clipped voice. "Her ideas about Kaltaarists are dangerous. All the more so since she returned from war a hero. Almost a legend."

"And whose fault is that," Grath asked, adjusting the lighting around the Traalk creeper. "You had your chance to get rid of her during the war, and you bungled it."

Raast was silent for a moment. "More accurately, the Vedrans did," she said coldly.

"And that rather clumsy attempt on her life only two days ago?"

"What am I expected to accomplish with agrarian rebels as my only agents? Had you allowed me to use my own staff, Kaylenn and her Kaltaarist whore would be dead now. More to the point, Prime Minister, can you afford to antagonize the Transtar Combine? The other conglomerates will not look kindly on such an example. Not even Transtar's competitors will be favorable to the precedent."

Grath clenched a fist in anger as she strode toward her liquor cabinet and fixed herself a strong drink. "I'm sick and tired of playing by their rules!" she shouted, pouring liquor into her glass. "They're bleeding our production worlds dry, the populations on the inner planets are starving, and the Combines tell me they'll solve the problem by expanding our frontiers into the neighboring star groups." She took a large swallow of liquor. It was dry and it burned her throat, but she needed it badly. "It's not enough I have to contend with pirates and insurgents in a dozen underfed systems. Now I'm expected to lead our people into another war!" She drained the glass. She took a deep breath, her head swimming. She clutched her chest, feeling the insufferably steady, continuous throbbing of her mechanical heart. A remarkable invention some Kaltaarist medical unit had contrived during the war, utilizing the principle of cybernetics Kralites had used in developing the robot bomb. She could still feel the shrapnel of the exploding bulkhead on the bridge of her command ship ripping through her original heart that day. The day her first one had died before her eyes.

"You must face reality, Prime Minister," Raast said with grim certainty. "You would never have been able to consolidate your power base after the war if the Combines had not manipulated the trade routes in your favor, to say nothing of the arms sales they arranged. And now, with the number of ministers they own body and soul—"

"Don't remind me! I'm to be their obedient dog, or they will destroy me." She poured herself a second drink, and offered one to Raast, who held up a hand, refusing. "I don't like the options I'm being offered, and I have no intention of accepting them! I prefer to broaden the field of play on my own terms."

"Your terms, or Kaylenn's?" Raast asked coldly.

Grath turned to glare at her. That usually intimidated most of her subordinates, but Raast held firm, her thin face rigid as her stance, her cold green eyes expressionless. "I am hoping that Kaylenn and the Transtar Combine cancel each other out! In the meantime...Kaylenn has offered me an interesting deal. In exchange for my official neutrality and unofficial military aid, she has promised to restore Zeln's agricultural production and offworld exports. If I could take credit for restoring the food shipments to the inner planets, that would win me many allies, and weaken the hand of the Combines."

"Dangerous," Raast grumbled.

"Risk is sometimes the price of survival," Grath said, sipping her second drink. "I learned that on the battlefront. You wouldn't know about that, since you were busy torturing captured spies back then." The other feme fought to repress a scowl, much to Grath's amusement.

"I am to support Kaylenn's little revolution, then?" she asked with cold sarcasm.

"Quietly, and at a distance," Grath replied. "Work

only through mercenaries.   Don't use your regular contacts on Zeln. I don't want Kaylenn discovering our ties to the Opposition. Or the reverse."

"On the subject of opposition parties, Prime Minister," Raast said, drawing her shoulders back with military formality, "I believe you should know that Vaaltyr is active here on Helkos again."

Grath sighed, sipping her drink. "Where?"

"Right here, in the capital. She's leading a rally in front of the Consulate. I think you'd better see for yourself."

Grath set down her glass and walked over to the computer terminal on her desk. She accessed the central information net, punching up local coverage. Half the room was filled with a shimmering three-dimensional hologram of political protesters brandishing symbolic tribal emblems and Kralite religious banners as they angrily chanted DEATH TO KALTAARISTS! DEATH TO KALTAARISTS! The capital security staff in their armored suits stood firm in a defensive perimeter around the heavily fortified Consulate building, their lasers at the ready.

"Daughters of Kral!" a young feme with flaming red hair cried, standing against the background of the Consulate facade. "The Kaltaarist filth has contaminated our society! The burden they place upon us has cost us dearly in the last war. Our leaders are weak and corrupt! They have allowed Kaltaarist weakness and perversity to infect us! To weaken us!"

Grath muted the sound and froze the image of the feme's face on close-up. Not particularly attractive, but striking in an odd way. Angry, penetrating blue eyes and short, tousled hair, the color of blood on fire. Grath accessed the computer archives, and the feme's service record appeared in midair beside the image of her angry face, scrolling up before Grath's eyes.

Vaaltyr. She had been a minor non-commissioned line officer during the war. Badge of valor for injuries sustained in combat. A good soldier. Or a reckless one. Overall, nothing particularly noteworthy. "Jail her," she said, deactivating the hologram. "And, in future, don't trouble me with rabble."

Chapter 23

Timeline: Kalthaar Experiment
Timeline Spatial: Production Zone Zed-4, Planet Zeln's Northern Continental Province, in the galaxy of Kalthaar
Timeline Chronological: The fourth millennium after the age of Kaarth, section point 122925

Kaylenn's shuttle flew low over a reserved tract of land a few miles from the chemical refineries. Mainly farmland with a bit of forest around it for the Kralines. Sparse and miserable land, Kaylenn thought to herself. "This is where your people were moved after Transtar seized your farms?" Kaylenn asked.

"Yes," Zelkys said dryly. "Those of us that chose to stay. Those are some of our living quarters, there." She pointed to a filthy little makeshift village of improvised dwellings and emergency military shelters clustered around a long, narrow building. Apparently a renovated storage facility. The shuttle set down at a landing pad surrounded by guard positions mounting outmoded laser turrets.

"If this is a trap," Kaylenn warned, looking at Zelkys and clutching Saaryth's hand.

"Don't worry," Zelkys said in a reassuring voice. "Zaard has said that no harm will come to you. We are simply protecting ourselves."

Saaryth stroked a comforting hand along Kaylenn's forearm. Kaylenn nodded to her and motioned for Zelkys to escort them off the shuttle. Zelkys looked a bit dubious as she stared at Saaryth. "I'm not sure it's a good idea for the Kaltaarist to accompany—"

"She stays with me," Kaylenn said firmly. She looked to Saaryth for agreement, and Saaryth nodded.

"As you wish," Zelkys muttered. She led them

through the shuttle's embarkation hatch and down the steps of the boarding ramp onto the dried, yellowed grass surrounding the village. Kaylenn stepped from the cool, fresh, air-conditioned interior of the shuttle into oppressive, hazy summer heat. She winced at the smell of the place. Improper sanitation. Sewage and garbage rotting in the sun, and the stench of noxious chemical waste filling the hot wind. A party of armed femes in worn, grimy workclothes greeted them. "Welcome home, Zelkys," one of them said. She looked even younger than Zelkys. "Which one of you is Kaylenn?"

"I am," Kaylenn announced, a bit insulted at such common treatment.

"Zaard is expecting you," the young one said. "Please accompany us."

Kaylenn glanced around at the others. Little more than children, some of them. But with faces hard as stone masks, fire burning in their eyes. "Lead on," she said.

Zelkys led Kaylenn and Saaryth inside the main building, the guards flanking them. Kaylenn looked around in the poorly lit, musty interior. Little more than a warehouse, really. Supplies. Workers moving about, most of them armed. Kaylenn and Saaryth were stopped and searched. Kaylenn fumed, but Saaryth, in her way, kept her calm. Zelkys, her young friend and two of the guards accompanied them into a lift. It took them down into a kind of subbasement; a network of gray metal corridors lit with fluorescent panels in the ceilings, armed femes standing guard every few yards. Zelkys led them down one corridor.

Kaylenn found herself in a kind of improvised military command bunker. Stockpiled weapons, explosives, communications and sensor equipment. "The Opposition has been generous, I see," she muttered in Zelkys's direction. "Where's Zaard?"

"Right here," one feme said, moving into the open. As she did, a number of lasers trained on Kaylenn and Saaryth. Zaard lifted a hand, ordering them to stand down. "So, this is the mighty Kaylenn," she remarked with an impudent gesture of her head. Kaylenn was struck by her beauty. Tall, lean and strong, with a graceful stance. Short, close-cropped raven hair framed her strong, handsome face and piercing dark blue eyes. Kaylenn had not felt this instantly drawn to any feme since her first meeting with Saaryth. Even through the arrogance of command this rebel wore, Kaylenn could sense a reciprocal attraction in those captivating eyes. Feeling a pang of guilt, Kaylenn averted her eyes.

"Yes, I am Kaylenn," she said haughtily. "This is my first one, Saaryth." She turned to her lover, laying a hand gently on her arm. Saaryth politely inclined her head to Zaard, who gave her a passing glance of undisguised distaste, and then turned her attention back to Kaylenn.

"Let us come directly to the point, Governor General," she said coldly. "What are your intentions for our territory?"

Kaylenn raised her eyebrows, drew a deep breath and sighed. "You're welcome," she said sarcastically. "Since we're being direct, let me say I had hoped for a bit more hospitality, considering you did try to kill me. I've risked a great deal to help your people."

"Have you?" Zaard almost laughed. "My people are dying by the day, Governor General! Your kind intervention has come a bit too late to save a great many of my sisters. You'll forgive me if I don't fawn with gratitude just yet."

Kaylenn was formulating a response, trying to decide just how much information to give up when

Saaryth suddenly spoke up. "How badly are your people suffering?" she asked with that instinctive compassion of hers. "This degree of toxicity must have contaminated most of the water table by now. That, combined with these living conditions must be causing high incidents of disease. I suppose there are quarantines in effect?"

Zaard stared curiously at her. Kaylenn could see she was also impressed by Saaryth's assessment. "Yes. Hundreds are dead of disease. Water, food...nothing's safe anymore. We've had to burn half our produce and close off the dead zone where the waste leaking into the groundwater is at its worst. Most of the arable land is gone. They're burning the bodies of the dead like kindling now!" Anger flashed in her eyes as her voice boomed.

Saaryth stepped forward. "I would like to see this 'dead zone' you mentioned," she said calmly.

"Why?" Zaard demanded.

"To assess the damage. Look for effective ways to heal the wounds. A logical place to begin an alliance is to collaborate in attacking the root cause of mutual problems, is it not?"

Zaard looked her over, apparently studying her closely. She glanced at Kaylenn. "I agree," Kaylenn said. "A logical place to start."

Zaard pondered. "All right."

Chapter 24

Timeline: Kalthaar Experiment
Timeline Spatial: Production Zone Zed-4, Planet Zeln's Northern Continental Province, in the galaxy of Kalthaar
Timeline Chronological: The fourth millennium after the age of Kaarth, section point 122925

Femes lay in rows of cots, tiny black flies buzzing about the open sores covering their arms and legs. Saaryth was horrified as she walked through the makeshift hospital with Kaylenn and Zaard. Her rapid breathing fogged the faceplate of the airtight protective suit she wore. A few medics wearing the same bulky yellow suits moved from cot to cot. Others carried the dead outside on stretchers. "Is this plague curable?" she asked the Kaltaarist physician walking along beside her.

"It's a cocktail of mutant viruses," the other feme said wearily. Even through the faceplate of her suit, her eyes betrayed many nights without sleep. "New variants appear faster than I can keep up with under these conditions." She waved a gloved hand across the filthy deathhouse that had been set up in a converted grain storage building. "These primitive drugs and incubators I'm forced to work with are all but useless." She groaned in plain disgust, the moans of the dying all around her. "If I had access to Kaltaarist viral labs and medications, I could deal with this outbreak effectively."

Saaryth looked at Kaylenn. "We've had some luck smuggling medical supplies in from Trynn."

"I could arrange to smuggle in a few supply shipments, I suppose." Kaylenn said.

"That's not enough," the doctor protested. "I need

proper laboratory facilities, and Kaltaarist genetics teams. If the necessary personnel and equipment could be flown in from the Trynn system—"

"Impossible," Kaylenn declared. "Government officials on a dozen planets have been executed just for smuggling Kaltaarist medicines. The public just won't stand for it."

"I'm not sure even my own people would," Zaard said with a deep sigh. "Many of them are old enough to remember how our farms had to struggle to survive against competition from Kaltaarist farming cooperatives. The massacres in my mother's time were what pushed the government to resettle the Kaltaarists on Trynn in the first place."

Saaryth looked at the doctor and nodded at her expression of disgust. "You hate us enough to die?" she asked Zaard.

The rebel leader looked around her and clenched a fist. "No, but it's hard. I'm sure your first one will agree."

Saaryth looked at Kaylenn. "Dead workers can't produce," she said. "Surely you can make the Prime Minister see that."

"She's barely tolerating us as it is! If I even mention Kaltaarist medicine, she's liable to switch sides. That helps no one."

"The agricultural trade is important to her. You said so yourself."

Kaylenn sighed. "Yes, and it looks like I may have promised her more than I can deliver."

A tree limb crumbled in Kaylenn's hand. The wood was like a brittle, calcifying paste. "All the vegetation is like this, for miles in every direction," Saaryth said beside her, "so the animal life is pretty much gone, of course. According to these chem readings on the soil samples tested," she drummed up the figures on a hand comp, "the water table now has a toxicity level well beyond what this biosphere can withstand." She stepped close beside Kaylenn, her voice muffled by her protective mask. "According to my Kaltaarist sources in the other five provinces, it's the same in every production sector the Combines have taken over. Between food chain and water contamination, and the spread of these mutant viruses, the entire planet will be affected within five years."

"How bad?"

"As a self-sustaining world with any kind of economic potential, Zeln will be finished in about ten to twelve years."

Kaylenn sighed, staring up at hazy yellow sunlight filtered through blackened, withered tree limbs. "No one in the Planetary Governor's office considered this when the land auctions were first proposed?"

Saaryth put a hand on Kaylenn's shoulder. "You said it yourself, love. Your people don't think like mine."

Kaylenn boiled in her protective suit. "Kelnaath and her Opposition friends just pocket their Combine money and move on to a comfortable early retirement on Helkos, or some pleasure world, while the rest of the population is left to scavenge through the Confederation systems. Indentured service. Mercenary work. Prostitution." She winced in disgust, looking at the devastation around her. "That's just the ones with money enough to get offworld at all!" The Kalthaar tribes were fast running out of frontiers, she sadly realized. Most of the habitable worlds in the known Galaxy were taken, the rest mined out and ruined. The empires were cramped and hemmed in now. Helkos and all the other major worlds would eventually have to be abandoned. New star groups to be explored. New hunting grounds, new empires. More of the same.

"Kaylenn," Zaard called out to her from a withered thicket nearby. "You might want to have a look at this." Kaylenn and Saaryth joined her, and she led them through the dying trees. "There," she said, pointing at a dying Kraline. It struggled feebly through the black mire, all six of its limbs scratching with pathetic weakness. Its mandibles opened and closed with excruciating slowness, its breath hissing out in gurgling, spitting gasps.

Kaylenn recalled the first time her mother had taken her to a state medical facility to watch sapien infants cut from the bellies of Kralines snared by femes from her cluster. She had been five years old then. She remembered hunting Kralines in her home village, just a few hundred kilometers from this spot. She remembered how swift and agile they were, how vicious when cornered. Those lightning-swift claws, snapping mandibles and burning acid spit had frightened her when she was a young feme. She still had the scar on her left arm and a bit of yellow freckling on the back of her hand from that acid. A souvenir of the first Kraline she had caught. She smiled as she recalled bagging the little devil in her net, fighting those clawed limbs, bracing the mandibles apart and binding the animal upside-down so its acid would drain out safely. She had been only fourteen then. She had held the Kraline up for the older kids to see. Her mother had been so proud.

Zaard prodded at the pitiful creature's mouth with a stick. It hissed and drooled, its mandibles clicking a bit. *Pathetic.* Zaard kicked the dying beast onto its back. It lay there squeaking, its legs twitching. Zaard knelt over it and drew a working knife from her belt. The Kraline gave out one short, loud squeal as she cut it open. Kaylenn nearly puked at the sight of the twisted, deformed sapien infant inside the Kraline.

Gray and already decaying, covered in dark, cloying gelatinous filth. Zaard stepped back, drew a hand laser and incinerated the abomination. Black smoke rose from its charred remains. "One in four are like this," Zaard grimly declared. "Even beyond the dead zone. And Kral Herself? She almost never lives to emerge from the cocoon, once the Kralines have fed."

Tears filled Kaylenn's eyes. She shut them tightly, hoping no one would see. She seized Saaryth by the arm and took her aside. "Is it too late?" she asked desperately, tightening her grip on Saaryth's arm. "Can Zeln still be saved?"

Saaryth looked at her. "Not unless you allow my people to come back here," she said quietly. "En masse, and with no limits placed on medicine or technology. There might still be time, but only if we begin now."

Kaylenn released her arm, turned and walked back to Zaard. "Zaard," she began calmly. "Zed-4 is yours." Zaard's mouth dropped behind her faceplate. "Effective immediately, I am declaring this sector an autonomous agricultural project. Your official title will be Production Administrator. This means, of course, full amnesty for you and all your people. All criminal warrants are, as of now, revoked."

Regaining her composure, Zaard looked at her suspiciously. "The price?"

"I need you to accommodate a Kaltaarist colony from Trynn."

"Colony?" Zaard shouted. "How large?"

"As large as needed to get the job done."

"We'll need to construct soil and water purification plants," Saaryth put in, stepping up beside Kaylenn. "Genetics labs. Large-scale molecular separators. This will be a full-scale terraforming project. Years in duration."

"We can't hide anything that big!" Zaard protested. "Kelnaath will never allow it! She'll have the combined armies of the other five provinces down on us!"

"I'll deal with Kelnaath," Kaylenn said.

Zaard sighed in frustration. "My own army may turn against me!"

"You have my army behind you, now," Kaylenn replied. "Between the two of us—the three of us," she amended, glancing at Saaryth, "we might have a chance of saving this planet. You've shown how clever you can be, Zaard. Prove you can be brave as well."

Zaard stared at the dead ground. She lifted her eyes and stared at Saaryth for a few moments. Then, she turned to Kaylenn. "Before I agree to anything, I want proof that these Kaltaarists are the miracle workers you claim them to be. None of them sets foot on my lands unless I know exactly what they plan to do and how, and how it will affect my people."

Kaylenn nodded, then turned to Saaryth. "Can you arrange this?"

"I believe I can," she replied.

"Then it is agreed," Kaylenn declared. "Zaard, you'll accompany Saaryth and me offworld. Select one of your lieutenants to command in your absence. I'll instruct my commander, Kolis, to obey her orders until we return. Agreed?"

Zaard stared at her. "Where are we going?"

"To Trynn, of course."

Chapter 25

Faln emerged from her prescient trance. "Oooh…" Faln nearly fainted as her mind withdrew from the time stream, her body shifting back into normal space.

"What did you see?" Ralyn asked her daughter, taking her face in her hands. "Tell me."

"Two planets. First, forests green and alive then deserts, cold and dead, then turning back to forests again. Then…it gets misty. Desert, forest. Forest, desert. People who should be alive are dead. Then, people I saw dead are alive. Why, mother?"

"You've found a focal point in the timeline," Ralyn explained, stroking Faln's face and looking into her wide blue eyes with wonder. The rarest of gems, a deciding moment in history, and, her daughter had found it. "Do you feel ready to go back in?" she asked hopefully.

Faln hesitated a moment, rubbing her forehead and sighing. "I guess."

"All right. Take my hands. That's it. Now, follow my thoughts back the way you came. Tell me what you see."

"A dead planet turning to forest. First, ice and dust. Then, grass. Trees. Rivers flowing…"

Chapter 26

Timeline: Kalthaar Experiment
Timeline Spatial: Planet Trynn's capital city, in the galaxy of Kalthaar
Timeline Chronological: The fourth millennium after the age of Kaarth, section point 122947

Kaylenn stood with Saaryth and Zaard at the viewport of Kaylenn's diplomatic space shuttle as it passed over the capital city of Saaryth's homeworld, Trynn. She could not believe her eyes. This was the capital of a world?

Through the cold, misty twilight landing lights flashed from the air traffic control towers ringing the circular structure of the main command and control complex. Rectangular projections jutted out across the rugged, icy ground. Smaller buildings resembling military barracks were positioned in neat geometric patterns between the extended wings, connected to the hub structure by pneumatic tubes which rung the great wheel like an array of perfect, delicate spokes. *All very precise and efficient. All utility and practicality,* Kaylenn reflected. *No art or style at all.*

The shuttle was cleared for landing and touched down on the landing pad at the center of the hub. As she disembarked, Kaylenn was struck by the conspicuous lack of ceremony. No honor guard, no music. The boarding ramp lowered onto an austere gray steel hangar deck. The only people present were three femes dressed in the traditional robes and cowls of Kaltaarist tribal counselors and priestesses.

"The feme in the blue cloak is Zaalyn, the First Planner," Saaryth whispered to her.

"That's the leader of a planet?" Zaard scoffed. "She doesn't look like much."

"Be quiet!" Kaylenn admonished in an angry whisper. "Saaryth, handle the formalities, please."

Saaryth led the way across the hangar. The welcoming delegation met them half way, stopping in the middle of the room, the two groups about three paces apart. Saaryth placed her hands over her heart, then extended them palms-up to the three, in the traditional Kaltaarist greeting between village elders or their representatives. "On behalf of Kaylenn, Governor General of the Northern Continental Province of Zeln: Greetings to the First Planner and good will to her people. I am the Governor General's acting representative, Saaryth of the Haleen Cluster in the Commune of Taark in the region of Draal." Saaryth sounded nervous, her voice quavering.

The three femes made the hand-to-heart sign to signify acceptance of the greeting. The one in the blue robe lifted her cowl and looked at Kaylenn. Kaylenn was struck by her appearance. She was old. In her sixties, perhaps, but with a strongly chiseled face and sharp black eyes which retained the commanding presence of authority. Long, silver-gray hair pulled straight back and fastened in a loose tail behind her head. The tattoo markings on her face were a bit more extensive and complex than Saaryth's. Signifying rank, Kaylenn guessed.

"On behalf of the allied communes of Trynn, I welcome you. I am Zaalyn, First Planner. This is Draeve, Planetary Trade Representative." The feme in the orange cloak to Zaalyn's left raised her cowl. Slightly younger. Long, black hair with streaks of silver. A cool, serious expression. Somewhat different tattoo markings. "And, Kren, our Chief Scientist." The stooped little feme in the maroon robe lifted her cowl. She was clearly the eldest of the three. Ancient, with thinning white hair and a thin, parchment-like face. But her eyes still gleamed with a keen awareness.

"Well, Saaryth," Zaalyn said, her voice a bit dry. Saaryth's eyes snapped up. "I am told this is your first visit home since the war."

Saaryth cleared her throat. "Yes, First Planner."

"I am gratified to see you have not forgotten all the traditions you were raised with." There was an accusing edge to her voice. Kaylenn glanced at Saaryth and saw her lower her eyes in apparent embarrassment, and awkwardly pull her robe and cowl over the gold necklace and earring Kaylenn had given her. Kaylenn gritted her teeth.

"Saaryth has been an invaluable aid to me on Zeln," she said pleasantly to the First Planner. "Her many talents are, no doubt, a tribute to the excellent teachers she had here. In fact, I must confess, were it not for her help and encouragement, I would never have tried my hand at statecraft. Or, interstellar commerce." She gave that one a moment to sink in. Zaalyn and the other two remained as calm and placid as ever. "That would have been tragic, wouldn't it?"

"Indeed," Zaalyn replied graciously. "Trynn, like Saaryth, has benefited greatly from your generosity, Governor General. In the material sense. However, we are here to discuss the price of these material benefits, are we not?" No anger in her eyes. An expression impossible to read. The infuriating honesty of these people made such telltale signs superfluous, of course.

"I prefer to think of it as cooperation, First Planner. Each of our communities has a need only the other can fill. Isn't it only sensible we collaborate?" Zaalyn looked surprised. That pleased Kaylenn. "You see, First Planner? Saaryth has had a positive influence on me." She glanced at her lover, and Saaryth looked away, hiding an embarrassed smile.

"Let us see just how 'positive.'" Zaalyn muttered.

"Draeve?"

The trade representative stepped forward and addressed Kaylenn. "You ask a great deal of us," she said in a cold, flat tone, her eyes steady and without expression. "A terraforming project on that scale would divert precious time and resources away from our ecological projects here on Trynn. In return, we would expect a legal guarantee of a permanent colony in Zed-4 and/or elsewhere on Zeln, as well as half the agricultural produce attributable to our labor."

"Half!" Zaard roared in anger, striding forward and standing beside Kaylenn. "Are you trying to insult us? We're offering to hire you as terraformers, not barter off half our profits."

"And you are?" Zaalyn asked.

"Forgive me," Saaryth interjected contritely. "This is Zaard, Production Administrator of Zed-4."

"I see." Zaalyn sighed. "Kren?"

The old feme stepped forward and produced a hand comp from beneath her robes. She drummed up a few figures on the device then spoke in a sharp, controlled voice much stronger than her appearance would suggest. "Based on the environmental and chemical data transmitted to us by our people on Zeln, we have assembled a theoretical scenario for reconstruction of that planet's ecosystem." She held up the hand comp. "Given the most conservative estimates of the time required, labor and raw materials—and the most generous estimates of your sector's productivity, we will barely regain our losses by taking half your produce. We cannot ask for less."

"I've wasted my time in coming to this ball of dust!" Zaard scowled in disgust and turned back toward the ship.

Kaylenn half-blocked Zaard's path and spoke quietly to her. "Think! What are you going home to?"

Zaard gritted her teeth. "We can't honor our offworld contracts if we give them half our produce, and you know it!"

"We're not honoring those contracts now. Zaalyn," she stepped toward the First Planner. "What if we alleviated your labor costs by bringing in Kralite workers from the inner planets?"

Zaalyn's eyes narrowed. "Prime Minister Grath would agree to this?"

"It's in her best interest. And, it would make our job easier; a sizable Kralite presence in Zed-4 would help us conceal the scale of your part in the project."

A scowl crossed Zaalyn's features for a fleeting instant. Then, she seemed to consider Kaylenn's offer. "It would mean training Kralites in the use of our equipment and methods. Kren?"

The old one shrugged. "It would cost us time, of course. Whether that loss of time would ultimately be balanced by increased productivity is difficult to say, without hard data." She grinned slyly. "There are, of course, cultural factors to consider. It is perhaps more a political decision than a technical one, First Planner."

Zaalyn shrugged and grimaced.

"I know how you feel," Kaylenn said with sincerity. "Before the war, I didn't believe Kaltaarists could learn Kralite skills. But I was proven wrong. We might surprise you."

The First Planner sighed. "Respectfully, Governor General, your people are not likely to be receptive. To expect Kralites to accept training and take orders from Kaltaarists..."

"Perhaps you should show us your facilities," Kaylenn suggested. "Then we'll decide."

Chapter 27

Timeline: Kalthaar Experiment
Timeline Spatial: Planet Trynn's capital city, in the galaxy of Kalthaar
Timeline Chronological: The fourth millennium after the age of Kaarth, section point 122947

Trynn was a dead world slowly coming to life. Before the Kaltaarist settlement was established there a generation earlier, the planet had been little more than a half-frozen rock in space. The atmosphere had been marginally breathable only at the equator, where it was just barely warm enough for water to exist in liquid form. Kaylenn was dumbstruck at what Saaryth's people had accomplished there in scarcely thirty standard years.

"We've depended mainly on offworld trade to acquire the necessary components to build this station, of course," Zaalyn explained as she stood with Kaylenn, Saaryth and Zaard on the control bridge of the orbiting solar station, looking down on Trynn from space. She signaled the station crew to adjust the large monitor screens receiving satellite views of the planet surface. One of many large-scale farming projects which were expanding in the equatorial regions appeared. Land which had once been frozen desert had been sectioned off into precise, geometric zones of cultivated greenery, rung by miles of solar collection grids. Flyers came and went from the habitation and production domes surrounding the farms.

Old Kren tapped a few keys on a computer terminal, and mathematical figures scrolled beside the view in two columns. "The column on the left indicates the cost of transporting essential nitrates and fertilizers," the aging scientist explained. "The column on the right indicates the total yield in bio-mass. Currently, we're showing a thirty percent gain on production. At present, of course, we only export raw botanical DNA offworld, but in approximately 2.122 years, we should be seeing subsistence farming in root crops and fruit trees. In 5.20 years, Trynn should be a thriving center of agricultural trade in the Helkos Confederation—and beyond, if the Confederation Council allows us to expand beyond this system. Zeln would be an important first step." She looked hopefully at Kaylenn.

"This station powers those solar conversion plants on the surface by microwave emission?" Kaylenn asked, fascinated by the sheer scale of it all.

"Yes," Zaalyn replied. "This one satellite sustains the four major agro projects in the western hemisphere. We have only one other such power station, in orbit above the opposite side of the planet."

"We should be able to afford two more such stations in the next five years," Draeve added. "Assuming Kren's projections are correct."

"Have they ever not been?" the old feme said through a smile of surprisingly healthy teeth.

During the war, Kaylenn had seen large-scale solar-powered space lasers used to destroy cities from orbit. The Kaltaarists had copied the technology and developed it in ways no Kralite government had ever even considered. "How is the land irrigated?" she asked.

"At present, we use flyers to import water from our ice extraction facilities at the poles," Zaalyn explained. "Not very efficient, but we're working toward making the planet's water supply more readily accessible." She directed Kaylenn's attention to another viewscreen and showed her the massive canal construction projects underway. Immense spider-shaped robot excavation machines cut their way through solid rock with laser beams, diverting the course of roaring underground rivers. Kaylenn did not even try to hide her awe at the level of robotic engineering. The machines obviously utilized the same type of positronic brains which guided the robot bombs. But the level of sophistication was unprecedented. "Long-range surface canals proved impractical because of the temperatures in the polar climes," Zaalyn went on. "We considered large-scale geo-thermal heating to melt the ice caps, but that approach was found not to be ecologically feasible in the long run. Sub-surface irrigation combined with low-yield geo-thermal manipulation proved the most effective approach."

"Those machines..." Kaylenn began.

"I'm sure you recognize some of your Kralite military technology, Governor General," Zaalyn said. "Robotic guidance systems. High-powered lasers. We've adapted the designs, and improved quality of performance considerably." Zaard scowled a bit.

"How have you managed atmospheric conversion?" Kaylenn asked.

Zaalyn led them to another viewscreen receiving satellite data from Trynn's northern polar region. Stretching across the vast white ice cap was a structurally precise network of sapien constructs, all interconnected with a huge central nexus, like the center of a spider's web. A thin, shimmering white geyser rose from the heart of the immense metallic web. Zaalyn ordered a closer view of the central installation.

It was a gigantic, roughly cylindrical apparatus, apparently a processing plant with a central chimney, spouting a monstrous plume of steaming white gases into the polar atmosphere. Smaller such geysers erupted from dome-shaped spouts positioned along the miles of gray metal tubes stretching across the ice sheet. Steaming white clouds obscured the scene, rain falling and freezing to glistening ice along the surface of the huge pipes. "The main converter taps the oxygen trapped in the ice cap and releases it into the atmosphere," Zaalyn explained. "The converter's power source is hydrothermal, of course, which also helps facilitate the production and purification of our water."

"The converter...it seems the same in principle as devices that sustained some of our emergency bases on asteroids during the war," Kaylenn recalled aloud. "Yes, I remember hearing some of your people helped our engineers design and build those shelters for us. But, the scale—"

"Necessary," Kren was matter-of-fact.

"How was it financed?" Zaard asked, casting an accusing eye at Kaylenn.

"We supply water and oxygen to passing Kralite ships, as well as a number of Kralite military outposts and mining settlements in the neighboring systems," Draeve replied. "The converter nearly pays for itself now. Once Trynn is at full productivity, we'll repay all debts."

Zaalyn directed Kaylenn's attention to a view of a somewhat different converter in a desert region. It looked something like a Kralite mining thruster, but much bigger. A jet of blue flame, like a gigantic acetylene torch roared from its huge spout. "We've adapted some of your mining technology in the southern region," Zaalyn said. "The operation pays for itself with mineral extraction, but its primary function is the mass production of carbon dioxide gas. Many of your large-scale Combine mining operations have destroyed entire planets. Depletion of atmospheric ozone shields on those worlds has caused planetary warming that wiped out agriculture and animal life. In the case of Trynn, of course, some amount of CO_2 in the upper atmosphere is badly needed right now to trap more of the sun's radiation and raise the temperature of this planet to an ecologically hospitable level. Once we've achieved a self-sustaining climate, of course, this operation will have to be dismantled."

"How can you just dismantle an entire mining operation?" Zaard demanded. "What about the owners? The investors?"

Draeve's facial expression twisted into one of revulsion. Kren giggled in amusement. Zaalyn sighed and cast her eyes up in an expression of—sadness? Exasperation? Condescension? Kaylenn could not tell. "That kind of planning—or rather lack of planning, is what has destroyed hundreds of your planets. We choose not to live that way. Instead, we choose to live."

"You mean you control the means of production," Zaard said in an accusing tone. "You decide, you give the orders, and your commune subjects just follow your orders like good little slaves?"

Zaalyn looked directly at Zaard. "Do you not control your people? Do you not enslave others for your own purposes?"

"That's different! My people respect me. I earned my position."

"As I have earned mine. The Communal Assembly of Planners elected me to this position because I was qualified to serve the interests of my people. The Bureau of Inspection monitors every one of my projects while it's still in the planning stage. The Assembly approves or, if necessary, modifies every plan—"

"A system where everyone is a slave!" Zaard shouted in angry derision. Several of the station techs looked up from their consoles. Saaryth looked deeply embarrassed. "Even its leader. You're like a colony of ants!"

"Interesting metaphor," Zaalyn said quietly with a look of mild sadness. "Ants and other such insects are burrowing creatures. Their interaction with the soil helps keep it fit for the sustenance of plant life, which in turn sustains larger parasites. Like sapiens." Zaard looked nauseated. She clenched a fist, and Kaylenn reflexively moved between her and Zaalyn. "I am told soil depletion is currently a key problem on your planet. Perhaps you'd like to inspect one of our soil conversion facilities?" Zaard looked into Zaalyn's eyes and relaxed, apparently interested. Saaryth was visibly relieved.

"Soil conversion at a molecular level," Kren explained as she walked along beside Kaylenn, Saaryth, Zaalyn, Draeve and Zaard through one of the many underground soil conversion facilities miles beneath Trynn's surface. Kaylenn looked along the seemingly endless rows of humming machines and coursing streams of blue-white energy flowing along the tunnels through which they walked. Kaylenn recognized the technology immediately. The same tachyon particle acceleration principle Kralites had long since developed for the purpose of propelling starships across the void. The Kaltaarists had found a way to harness that power for somewhat more constructive uses, and on an inconceivably vast scale.

"This looks like a larger version of the Braal-class tachyon accelerator," Kaylenn remarked.

"Essentially it is," Kren explained. "With a few modifications. We've adapted your forcefield technology to help channel and control the energy flow."

Kaylenn tried to conceal her awe. "Impressive, but the conduction elements in these tachyon generators burn out quickly—not to mention overall maintenance costs. To use them in continuous operation on this scale can't be very economical."

"Your conduction elements are substandard," Draeve remarked matter-of-factly. "We've upgraded your design and made it more efficient. Ours lasts much longer." She handed Kaylenn a hand comp displaying the computer specs for the generator. "As for maintenance costs," she shrugged and smiled slightly for the first time in Kaylenn's presence. "I think the cost analysis I've prepared for you speaks for itself."

The sheer organization, Kaylenn mused as she tried to process everything she had seen in the few short days since arriving on Trynn. The Kaltaarist spirit she had come to know during the war. This, however, was the spirit given flesh and armor. These people lived for each other, she realized. Each worker and administrator labored for the commune, not for her own profit. It wasn't like a production camp, with guards pointing lasers and neural whips. It seemed to come from inside each feme who labored in each tunnel, each farm, each converter base and each space station. She asked herself what spirit drove them. Then she remembered her visions while being tortured in the camp. A faint chill ran through her, and she looked at Saaryth. Saaryth gently ran a hand along her arm, as though sensing her thought and sharing it.

They reached what looked like an airlock, and Kren instructed them to seal the oxygen helmets of their airtight isolation suits. Stepping through the airlock, Kaylenn and the others entered a large chamber which resembled a combination factory complex and laboratory. Raw soil poured from large spouts onto conveyor belts which carried them through a chemical treatment apparatus. A technician in a white isolation suit handed Kren a hand comp. The chief scientist called up the latest chemical readings on the ongoing soil conversion. "Good. The chemical breakdown is occurring at the rate expected, and the raw organic deposits in the third rock layer are as rich as the preliminary samples suggested. Now let's see if the genetics team is having as much luck."

Teams of sapiens in shiny white plastic suits worked around long tables of sealed transparent cases filled with soil samples. Reaching into the glass cases with a variety of cybernetic manual extensions, they added chemicals, ran tests and extracted samples. Some of the soil cultures pulsed with activity, as though some kind of burrowing life were crawling through them. Others sustained a variety of exotic plant life. Strangely shaped leaves and oddly colored flowers being pollinated by an assortment of flying and crawling insects Kaylenn had never seen before: four-inch, six-winged green flies flew among long, fuzzy-gray creatures with a thousand legs.

"Genetically engineered mutant insect life," Kren explained. "We've experimented with thousands of species variants that we collected on Zeln and transplanted here when we were first exiled by your people." She spoke calmly, Kaylenn noted. Without bitterness. "We try to design and breed the most efficient animals to pollinate the mutant plant species and enrich the nutrients in the processed soil, of course. However, our work begins on a much smaller scale, as you see here." She called their attention to a computer-generated 3D hologram of a strain of bacteria viewed through a super microscope positioned over one of the soil cultures. "We've deployed billions of mutant bacterial strains, trying to spawn increasingly successful hybrid species to energize the soil of this planet."

"Could you develop vaccines for the plagues?"

Zaard asked hopefully, an edge of desperation to her voice.

Kren shrugged. "Given time and proper facilities, and the opportunity to study the environmental conditions firsthand...I believe we could. Yes."

The flash of excitement in Zaard's eye was brief, but clear. "Interested, Zaard?" Kaylenn asked.

"We might be able to reach accommodation," Zaard said in a subdued voice. "We'll have to work out the labor problem, of course—with or without offworld help, and then come to an acceptable profit-sharing deal. Yes...I think we can do business."

Chapter 28

Timeline: Kalthaar Experiment
Timeline Spatial: Planet Trynn's capital city, in the galaxy of Kalthaar
Timeline Chronological: The fourth millennium after the age of Kaarth, section point 122947

"You were magnificent," Saaryth whispered joyously as she and Kaylenn 'celebrated' in the quarters Zaalyn had provided them on the planet surface.

Kaylenn playfully nipped at her neck and pulled the tangled sheets around their intertwined bodies. "Shall I consider that praise from my teacher?"

"No," Saaryth said with a smile. "Only this." She kissed her, their breasts pressing closely. She stroked her hand slowly down the length of Kaylenn's body and, with her usual artful finesse, found her way inside. Kaylenn moaned in deep pleasure, and returned the favor. They lay together for a time, enjoying the warmth of each other's arms. "Do you believe Zaard will come around in the end?"

"It won't be easy. I don't envy her the task of rallying the workers in Zed-4 once the operation there begins. But I think I can get Grath on our side. That's the important thing."

"Still...What if Zaard turns on us a few months or a year from now, and tries to nationalize our technology?"

"Zaalyn seems ready to take that chance." Saaryth suddenly slipped out of bed and pulled on a robe.

"Love?" Kaylenn got up, put on her own robe and joined Saaryth at the window. Saaryth pressed a button, electrically opening the curtains. The sun was low and pale in Trynn's cold glassy sky. The full-length window looked out on long rows of genetically engineered plants, their leafy stalks swaying in a gentle breeze. Agrobots wheeled along the metal tracks between the rows, their long, delicate metallic limbs weeding, mulching and watering with computerized precision. Kaylenn gently pressed against Saaryth from behind, her arm around her waist. "You all right?" she asked softly, brushing aside a tress of Saaryth's long, coiling dark hair and kissing her on the neck.

"Zaard desires you very much," Saaryth said flatly. "I can tell. And, I know you feel the same way about her."

Kaylenn sighed in guilt and frustration. She took Saaryth by the shoulders and turned her toward her. Her face was calm and still. No sign of anger or fear. Only resignation. "Is that it? Love..." she kissed her on the lips. "I will never betray you. Could you think otherwise after all we've been through? Lust passes. It's nothing. What you and I have built..." She reached for Saaryth's face.

"I think you should go to her."

Kaylenn withdrew her hands. "What?" She stared at her lover in disbelief. "Saaryth..." she drew back a step. "There's nothing I need or want to work out of my system, if that's—"

"She wants you. We can use this to our advantage."

Kaylenn stared at her, a rancid taste in her mouth. "You mean, lie to her? Make her think I'm betraying you?"

"Tell her whatever you like. Tell her I have consented. Or, that I always yield to your will in such matters. I'll even join the two of you, if she wants me. I believe she does. I can tell. She masks it beneath her anger, but it's there."

Kaylenn felt nauseous. Three years of war...the

camp...four years together on Zeln, and now she was looking at a stranger. An alien. "What is this? Are you doing this to punish me? How can you even suggest—"

"We've done it before. It's how we survived the camp."

"That was different!"

"How? You said yourself this was war."

"I was wrong," she said quietly. Those words did not come easily to her. "You showed me that."

"No. I just taught you different tactics. It's time for your next lesson."

"I won't do it! I'd rather face Zaard in battle some day than—"

"Are you lying to me now, or to yourself?!" Saaryth shouted, catching Kaylenn off-guard. "You know you want to."

"I'm not an animal!" She turned and paced. These Kaltaarist quarters were infuriating. No liquor. No artificial stimulants of any kind.

"Is your pride more important to you than the future of two planets?"

Kaylenn spun, her fists clenched in frustration. "And which of those planets do you represent, Saaryth? You've been home one day and already you've forgotten what we were to each other?"

Saaryth's expression softened as she approached. "Kaylenn...I love you. That can never change. I am your first one. I am also, in my heart, a Kaltaarist. But I speak as one who wants you to succeed. You want to save your homeworld. I want to save mine. The two are not in conflict." She placed her hands softly against Kaylenn's face. "You needn't feel any guilt for your part, or fear of what I might feel." She paused, as though considering what she was about to say. "I have discussed this with Zaalyn, and she feels-"

Kaylenn pushed her hands aside, horrified, and

struck her hard across the face with the back of her hand. "Whore! You...you told that witch about me? About *us!*" She paced and clenched her fists in fury. Every nightmare she had dreamt over the past seven years was coming true. She felt like a wretched fool. How could she have been deceived for so long? "How dare you?" She grabbed Saaryth by the hair and hurled her to the floor. "You used me! You'd give me to Zaard as a bribe? *Me?*" She was screaming hysterically, her eyes filling with tears. *Damn, the weakness! This for a whore? A damned, deceiving witch of a whore.*

"I didn't use you," Saaryth said, getting up slowly and wiping the blood from her mouth, her voice shaky. "I'm betraying Zaalyn now by telling you this."

"One betrayal after another," Kaylenn raved, arms waving, a mock smile crossing her tear-streaked face. She could not even look at Saaryth. "A whore among whores!"

"Stop it!" Saaryth roared. Kaylenn turned. There was a ferocity rising in Saaryth's eyes that Kaylenn had never seen before. "Who are you to judge me? You choose to be a killer rather than a seducer, and that makes you noble?" Her teeth were bared. "But you are both killer and seducer, aren't you?" Her voice was shrill and wild, her fists clenched as she circled Kaylenn. "Whore? Yes, I was your whore, wasn't I? I was your whore! I killed for you! I betrayed all I was! I abandoned the people who raised me!"

"I loved you!"

"Did you? You brought me into your world, made me into your property..."

"Liar! I loved you. I would have died for you!"

"But not lived for me! Not in this world."

"There's no place for me here!"

Saaryth spat blood onto Kaylenn's robe and laughed mockingly. "No place for you here? Proud warrior, no place for her in a world of whores and drudges! Except me -- there was always a place for me in your world, wasn't there? As your concubine!"

Kaylenn hit her again.

Saaryth's eyes flared, and she attacked. A blow to Kaylenn's face, then a knee to her ribs, and a sweeping kick to her legs, knocking her off her feet. Flat on her back, Kaylenn landed a kick to Saaryth's stomach, then rolled. She stood, and Saaryth charged at her, screaming wildly. They fought, practiced blows and combat training quickly giving way to blind animal rage. They wrestled, clawing and biting. Kaylenn tasted blood.

They battered each other until they both lay on the floor, gasping and moaning in pain. Her rage spent, her body covered in sweat and her hands and face wet with her blood and Saaryth's, Kaylenn lifted her throbbing head and saw Saaryth on her hands and knees, obviously exhausted, yet still sobbing in helpless rage. Kaylenn tried to embrace her, but Saaryth lashed out with her fists, feebly thrashing. Kaylenn forced herself to lay back under her, her arms folded behind her back, and took the punishment. Exhausted at last, Saaryth collapsed on top of her, tears flowing from her eyes down Kaylenn's neck. "I don't know who I am anymore!" she screamed hoarsely through the tears. "What in the black void am I but what you've made of me? Damn you!"

Kaylenn wrapped her arms around Saaryth and held her, their tears merging. "Saaryth...I'm yours. I can't remember what I was before I knew you. Nothing. A stupid, empty dream that was more my mother's than my own. I was a ghost. A reflection, a...shadow. Then you came, and I was alive! Everything was different from what I'd always believed it could be. You made me, Saaryth. Can't you see that? I'm nothing without you. I am sorry." She cried, running her fingers through Saaryth's hair. "I am sorry I wasn't there for you when I should have been. But I'm here now, in your world. And I am yours. Tell me what to do."

Saaryth looked at her. Her cheek was bruised and swelling, her forehead bleeding profusely, but she looked deeply into Kaylenn's eyes and stroked her face. "Tell me why you're so afraid," she said in a raw, gravelly voice. "No more lies. Tell me what you're afraid of."

"Remember the light, forget the shadows." Her eyes stung with tears. "You've come back to the light. I'm just a passing shadow, like Zaard."

Saaryth closed her eyes. "You are blind... all this time and you still don't know." She opened her eyes. "You are my light, Kaylenn. Trynn is a place of shadows without you. I knew that the moment I met you. I tried to deny it. Repress it. I was terrified, but I couldn't lie to myself. You're part of me. If you die, I die."

Kaylenn wiped the tears from Saaryth's eyes. She tried to kiss her, but bruises and loosened teeth made that impossible for both of them. "Ohhh..." she groaned, licking her swelling lip.

"I'll signal for a medibot," Saaryth muttered, wincing in pain as she slowly stood. "Don't worry. No one will know."

Kaylenn sighed, joy and agony mixing inside her. "Why do I always end up battered and bloody after committing to you?"

"I'm expensive," Saaryth said with a pained smile as she reached for the com panel on the wall. "The best whores always are."

Kaylenn began to laugh, then clutched her side and moaned in pain. Three cracked ribs. Maybe this was war, after all.

Chapter 29

Timeline: Kalthaar Experiment
Timeline Spatial: Planet Trynn's capital city, in the galaxy of Kalthaar
Timeline Chronological: The fourth millennium after the age of Kaarth, section point 122957

Zaard drove her steel-tipped spear straight down as Kaltaari bucked under her feet, the huge animal throwing her off balance. Her spear-point lodged between the beast's armored scales as her feet slipped out from under her, and she fell.

She clutched her cable and locked the pulley. The nylon rope caught and pulled tight. She dangled from the grappling hook embedded in Kaltaari's flesh, just below the beast's third dorsal spine. The animal squawked and shambled about, the jungle shaking under its massive weight. The other femes in the hunting party either swung helplessly from their climbing ropes or helped each other over the razor-sharp spines along the great one's back, making for Her tiny, vulnerable brain. Zaard cursed as she tried futilely to snag one of the beast's scales with her metal pick-ax. "Oh, Kral, no," she whispered in fear and anger as the grappling hook began to give way.

"Zaard...catch," Kaylenn shouted to her from a secured position on the animal's flank. She tossed a rope-end with her free hand, her pulley spinning as the rope reeled down toward Zaard. Zaard caught it and swung just as her own rope gave way. A sharp-edged scale narrowly missed her leg, she braced her boots against Kaltaari's hide and pulled herself up, hand-over-hand, Kaylenn anchoring her above.

She reached Kaylenn, their hands clasping together on the steel piton that held them to the animal's side. "Thanks," she gasped, Kaylenn smiling at her, their faces nearly touching. Another rope coiled down from still farther above, and Kaylenn seized it.

"Grab hold," she grunted, starting the steep climb toward Kaltaari's back. Zaard looked up and saw Saaryth anchoring the rope, secured by a line looped around a two-meter dorsal spine. Zaard grumbled resentfully under her breath. "Come on," Kaylenn yelled down to her impatiently. Reluctantly, Zaard followed her up the rope. At the top, Saaryth and Kaylenn both reached down to her, offering her their hands. It felt humiliating, this...this charity. But a part of her wanted to reach out to Kaylenn. And, though it pained her to admit it, to Saaryth as well.

Pulling her to a standing position on Kaltaari's back, Saaryth handed Zaard a new spear. The gesture surprised her, but she accepted it. Kaltaari charged on through the jungle, trees crashing down before the armored behemoth. Zaard fell to her belly to avoid a falling tree-limb crashing across the monster's towering spines. Kaylenn and Saaryth huddled in close, protecting her as leafy branches shattered on top of them. Instinctively, she shielded both of them as best she could.

The rest of the hunting party sank their pitons and secured their lines, forming a living chain down the length of the animal's back, making straight for the brain. Zaard took the lead as she, Kaylenn and Saaryth made their way down the line of femes to their target. The others supported her as she advanced. What kind of people were these? They fought bravely, yet submitted to others. Cooperated, yet with no leader. She reached the brain case. Her old spear was still lodged where she had left it. Two other hunters dug in with pick axes and pried apart two armored scale plates, exposing the soft, pulsing orange flesh of the nerve stem below.

She aimed her spear tip at the target. She braced her feet, and, with Kaylenn and Saaryth behind her, she screamed and charged. All three of them moved as one, their combined strength driving the spear tip into the pulpy flesh of the exposed nerve, dark blood gushing from the breach. Kaltaari roared and staggered, crashing headlong into a huge tree. Zaard was thrown careening forward. She expected her brains to be dashed out the next moment. Her line snapped taught and pulled her back, her harness biting painfully into her shoulder. She turned her head to look back. Kaylenn, Saaryth and the others worked together to pull her back from the edge.

Kaltaari's mournful wail filled the air, and Zaard felt the huge beast shifting under her. Falling. "Brace for the drop!" Saaryth shouted. With practiced skill, the Kaltaarist hunters laid flat between the dorsal spines, quickly securing themselves with pitons and cushioning each other with their padded suits. Kaylenn and Saaryth secured themselves and pulled Zaard down between them. Cushioned between their bodies, she held tightly to both of them until she felt every bone in her body shake with the thunderous crash which followed. For a moment, her mind swam through space and star fields. Regaining her senses, she struggled to her feet and found herself upon Kaltaari's dead bulk.

Celebratory songs of victory and new life filled the air as grappling hooks snagged the scales of the fallen beast and workers from the nearby village clambered up ropes onto the giant carcass. Two of them marked off a wide, rectangular section of the animal's side, scanning with sonic probes. "Many, and strong," one of them announced happily, lifting her headphones. The others all cheered, Kaylenn included. Working with polished efficiency, the Kaltaarist laborers activated large-scale sonic blades and cut neatly and precisely along the lines laid out for them. Others sank grappling hooks at points along the incisions and attached ropes, all the while singing their work ballads.

The workers grasped the ropes as the harvesters stood by with their laser scalpels and swaddling cloths. Trains of femes stretched out the ropes on both sides of the animal and climbed back down to the ground in their spiked boots, their combined weight pulling open the two great flaps of the sectioned womb. Zaard looked down into the interior of the animal she had just killed, and her jaw dropped in astonishment. A multitude of sapien infants, crying and reaching up out of the bubbling, pinkish ooze. One by one, the harvesters extracted them from the womb, skillfully cutting their many umbilical links, then wrapping them in clean cloth. Saaryth cradled one of the newborns in her arms and walked toward Zaard. "Here," she whispered, smiling warmly as she offered the infant to Zaard.

"Mine?" Zaard asked quietly, confused.

"Ours," Saaryth said happily and with a slight laugh, glancing back at her many sisters caring for her/their many daughters. Zaard carefully took the little one in her strong arms. She looked down into the tiny face. The baby cried in the unfamiliar cold, her eyes not yet open. Zaard held her gently, feeling the new life against her beating heart. It filled her as songs of sisterhood filled the air around her. She could not speak.

"Kral!" one of the femes shouted from the ground. Zaard looked down, and her blood froze. There, clawing through the jungle with demonic speed, like a gigantic spider, was Kral, the Mother/Destroyer. Her deadly mandibles snapped. She lunged, tearing off the head of a feme who attacked Her with a pick ax. Her lethal acid spit killed two more who attacked with their grappling hooks. Spears rained down upon Her as She effortlessly clambered up the body of Kaltaari on her six clawed limbs. Zaard had pictured facing this a thousand times, but not like this. Not here.

She handed the baby in her arms to a worker and picked up a spear. "Distract Her," Kaylenn ordered, taking a spear and attacking Kral from the right. Saaryth attacked from the left. The other hunters thrust at the monster's hind and flanks with their spears, drawing Her attention away from the babies while the workers took them to safety. Zaard ducked to avoid Kral's acid spit and got in under Her guard, stabbing upward into Her huge, sucking mouth. The monster shrieked in pain and slashed at her with her forward claws.

The padded shoulder and sleeve of Zaard's suit were ripped open, a deep gash appearing in her shoulder, the pain lancing to the bone. In desperation, she threw herself under Kral, crawling beneath Her belly to escape the reach of those deadly claws. She pulled a piton from her belt and drove it into Kral's hard, scaly underbelly. The monster shrieked in anger and clambered around, trying to get the prey under Her in Her grasp. Zaard held firm to the piton, anchoring herself to Kral's belly and gouging with a grappling hook at the weak spots about the creature's legs.

The piton was jarred loose, and she fell. Rolling and crawling as quickly as she could over Kaltaari's jagged scales, she slipped clear of Kral. Reaching back for her spear, she saw Kaylenn anchored atop Kral's back, striking with a pick-ax, blinding the monster's many flaming green eyes. Saaryth and another feme stabbed at the creature's underbelly with spears while the others sank grappling hooks into Kral's legs and attached climbing ropes. Once the lines were secure, they all went over the edge of Kaltaari's gut together, their weight dragging the devil toward the edge. Kaylenn jumped from Her back, landed on her feet and rolled with the fall. One of the workers tossed her a spear, and she charged at Kral's front, adding her strength to that of the other two already trying to lever Her over the edge.

Zaard joined in, charging the beast with a war cry rising from her gut. She joyously drove the spear into the soft flesh between two of the monster's legs and drove in hard as the femes on the ground pulled in trains, their ropes stretching taught. Kral shrieked as She was pulled over the edge and fell crashing to the ground. Kaylenn, Saaryth and the other hunter jumped from Kaltaari's side onto Kral's belly, driving in with their spears. Zaard followed their example. She landed on the pliant, rubbery surface, digging her spearhead into the tough hide under her boots. Their combined weight kept Kral trapped on Her back, all six of Her limbs thrashing wildly.

Workers held Kral's limbs down with their grappling hooks and ropes while others cut them off one by one with their sonic blades. Zaard and the others stabbed and stabbed while the workers on the ground around them cut into all of Kral's weak spots at once. Soon, Kral shivered, squawked out Her last breath, and died. Zaard was numb, the reality of what had just happened slowly beginning to sink in as one of the workers handed Saaryth a sonic blade. Saaryth cut open Kral's belly, freeing the sapien infant within. She pulled the crying, bloodied baby from the monster's womb and cut the thick umbilical cord, cradling the child in her arms. As Kaylenn put her arm around Saaryth's shoulders, Zaard was dumbstruck.

The daughter of Kral had been born before her eyes. Pulled from the Mother/Destroyer's womb by a

Kaltaarist! And...whose daughter was she? She belonged not to Zaard, or Kaylenn, or even Saaryth, but to the entire village. No more or less so than all of the other infants they had won here today. Zaard sank to her knees on Kral's belly, slowly lowering her spear and letting it fall from her numbed hands. Everything she knew was gone. She no longer knew who she was.

Zaalyn stood before Zaard's interface couch. Adjusting the electrodes on Zaard's forehead, she checked the brainwave scanner monitoring the virtual reality simulation. Zaard was deep in the computer-generated world of the great hunt. Zaalyn saw one tear run down the feme's strong face.

"She fought well," old Kren said, smiling as she stood beside Zaalyn.

"The purpose of this simulation was not to test her fighting ability," Zaalyn sighed, slightly irritated. As brilliant a scientist as Kren was, and as invaluable her services, Zaalyn still found her impudent attitude quite annoying at times.

"Yes, yes, I know, First Planner," the wrinkled old crone chirped out condescendingly. "That's why I designed the program schematic to measure her emotional reactions to the hunt, and in particular to Saaryth and her...first one, Kaylenn."

"And the results?"

"Quite promising," she said, handing Zaalyn a hand comp.

Zaalyn looked over the computer breakdown of Zaard's evolving emotional pattern and nodded approvingly. "She's taken the first step. It could go either way now." She stepped over to Saaryth's interface couch, pausing briefly first at Kaylenn's. She glanced at the Kralite and fought off an involuntary twinge of resentment. Then she studied Saaryth's unconscious face intently. "Our fate may rest with you now," she whispered. "I hope you still remember who you are."

Chapter 30

Timeline: Kalthaar Experiment
Timeline Spatial: Production Zone Zed-4, Planet Zeln's
Northern Continental Province, in the galaxy of
Kalthaar
Timeline Chronological: The fourth millennium after
the age of Kaarth, section point 122959

"Get those shields in place!" Kolis screamed over the explosions and hum of laser fire all around her. She heaved the headless body of the sky gunner out of the turret control seat and took her place.

Lowering the scanner headset over her eyes, she brought the immense laser cannon on line with manual control, disconnecting the computer. She preferred her own touch any day. The turret swiveled beneath her on its hydraulic turn-table, the cannon elevating as she adjusted the attitude control. Against the black background of the VR viewer, she saw the three triangular red blips of the enemy flyers complete their turn and swing around for another pass. "That's right, little birds...stay together...just a bit closer..." She fired, just as they were about to enter range.

The beam intersected the first blip. She heard a thundering explosion overhead and her troopers cheering as the first blip disappeared. She adjusted the cannon's angle while still firing, and swung the beam, taking out the second blip. Another explosion in the sky and more cheers. The third blip changed course, escaping. Kolis angrily pounded in new targeting codes and swung the beam as quickly as she could, but she only managed to clip the target as it dropped sharply below the cannon's field of fire.

Kolis lifted the VR headset and saw the enemy fighter spinning in, a trail of black smoke behind it. The damaged flyer fired its lasers, twin beams of bluish light lancing down at Kolis's position. Explosions ripped the ground around the shield generators. "Evacuate!" Kolis screamed as she jumped from the turret. "Evacuate now!" The others ran from their positions. One of Kolis's troopers remained behind at a power unit, attempting to make the electrical contact which would close the circuit and activate the shield wall. "I said evacuate!" One bolt hit the power unit. A blinding explosion threw Kolis from the turret platform. Blackness closed over her.

The pain and heat of a raging fire brought her around. Her arm and shoulder were numb. She was dimly aware of the enemy fighter crashing somewhere in the distance, and prayed to Kral the witch had not had time to eject. She looked down and saw the smoldering shrapnel lodged in her shoulder. She realized if not for her body armor, it would have gone straight through the bone. No time to even try extracting it. She took a painkiller from her field kit and jabbed it into her carotid artery. She heard the laser fire converging on the perimeter. The enemy was bringing up its hovertanks, now that the shield was down.

She cursed as she shifted her laser from her shoulder, connecting the power lead as best she could with her one good arm, and raised her platoon commanders on her helmet radio. "Kalmyn...take the left flank. Tryss...take the right. Keep low, sweep forward, and fire at will. We can't hold this position, and we can't retreat, so dive down their throats and cut the witches apart from the inside out!" She joined them, cursing as she thought of Kaylenn's parting orders. She hated herself for what she was doing. She was sending young femes to die in a hopeless cause. Stupid waste! While the Governor General was where?

On Trynn, with her Kaltaarist whore and rebel ally! She cursed herself for having let it come to this. She had been so stupid! Time-honored loyalty had finally failed her. She should have seen Kaylenn for the traitor she was and betrayed her to the Planetary Governor when she had had the chance! Now it was too late, she reminded herself, focusing her anger on the enemy. Surrender meant execution for her and all her troopers. Might as well go down fighting. She would face Kral and every goddess with head held high! She spoke through her radio again. "Daaryn...take a demolition squad into the refineries. The minute those witches try to occupy them, blow the generators and kill them all!"

A dozen black-armored hovertanks swept across the gray, dusty plains, some bearing the white-and-gold emblem of Zeln's Planetary Governor, others marked with the blue-and-white emblem of the Southern Continental Province. Kolis's few remaining laser batteries took out two of them, their fuel pods exploding in beautiful red fire balls. The rest of the tanks fired, their beams lancing out and obliterating the last real defense Kolis had. She did not bother to look as she heard the power packs of the laser batteries exploding, and the screams of the gunners as they died. She and her foot soldiers seized those few precious seconds the gunners had bought them and charged forward, screaming in rage, racing to get in under the range of the enemy lasers. Some were sliced cleanly in two as the enemy hovertanks swept the field with their beams.

Kolis let her rage explode as she dropped and fired from her side, her beam rupturing the fuel pods of an enemy tank. She rolled as the hovertank's belly passed about two feet above her, the vehicle crashing in flames somewhere behind her. About half her company made it into the thick of the hovertank swarm. For a few minutes, it felt like easy pleasure. Hovertanks could not fire at sapiens running on foot at close quarters without hitting each other. Her troopers laughed as they swept the underbellies of the hovertanks, blowing out their fuel pods. Some exploded outright, the flames and shrapnel taking out some of Kolis's troops. Others managed to land while in flames. As the boarding ramps lowered and the enemy piled out, Kolis and her troopers joyfully picked them off, cutting them to bits as they ran coughing from the smoky interiors of their tanks.

The moment passed of course, as the surviving hovertanks pulled back and achieved positions from which they began effortlessly picking off her troopers like flies. Nearby, beyond the smoke and fire and dead bodies, Kolis saw enemy troop carriers touching down. As their boarding ramps lowered and a hundred armored femes with lasers piled out and charged, she knew it was over. She swung her laser toward them, gritting her teeth and preparing to run to her death. She could not believe her eyes as the troop carriers exploded in flames, taking the enemy troops with them. The wave of heat coming from that massacre hit her face, searing her eyes. Over the roaring flames, she made out small combat flyers whose insignia she did not recognize. Mercenaries, perhaps, but allies in any case.

She turned back toward the hovertanks, and was astonished to see them exploding one by one, cut to bits by laser fire from femes on jet skimmers. Zaard's people, she realized at once. Those young rebs she had dismissed as sorry misfits. They shrieked and cheered as they weaved between the slow hovertanks like demons in flight, hand lasers cutting fuel pod shielding at close range. The one apparently leading the attack was either fearless or certifiably insane. She screamed joyously, carrying on like an entertainer doing daredevil stunts as she rocketed about the field, scoring hit after hit.

Apparently fired by the shift in the tide, Kolis's troops renewed their attack, charging the tanks and taking them out while the rebels drew their fire. Shaking off her numbness, Kolis joined in, destroying another tank as it turned to fire. The other tanks were in retreat. They flew out of her people's range, only to be blown up from the air by strafing laser fire from the merc flyers. Before she knew what had happened, the battle was over. Kolis found herself surrounded by her cheering, joyful troops. The merc flyers roared overhead, turning and firing a few laser bursts in a grandstanding gesture. The jet skimmers set down nearby, and the young femes piloting them disembarked, hooting and shrieking as they pulled off their helmets. Little more than children, some of them.

Kolis and some of her troopers approached the rebel leader. Kolis recognized her as Zelkys, the young feme she had arrested and nearly killed several weeks earlier for trying to assassinate the Governor General. She looked at Kolis and smiled, wiping the sweat and grime from her face. "So good to see you again, Commander Kolis," she said impudently, with a bit of a mock salute, some of the other young femes around her giggling as they clapped her on the shoulders.

"You heal fast," Kolis muttered, looking her over, noticing the scars on her face and remembering the day she had put them there.

"You should feel damned lucky your aim wasn't better the last time we met, or I wouldn't have been here to save your ass!" The others laughed out loud.

Kolis nodded, grinning involuntarily. "You did damned well. You all did..." she began to feel a bit light-headed. The cheering grew faint as the fires began to swirl around her.

"Syr?" one of her troopers asked from somewhere in the distance. She felt herself falling. She was dimly aware of hands...many hands...her soldiers...helping her to the ground, laying her down. Zelkys bent over her, checking her wounds. Oddly enough...the last thing she noticed before blacking out was how pretty the rebel was, scars and all.

Chapter 31

Timeline: Kalthaar Experiment
Timeline Spatial: Planet Helkos, in the galaxy of
Kalthaar
Timeline Chronological: The fourth millennium after
the age of Kaarth, section point 122959

"Kelnaath is not happy," Raast grumbled as she joined Prime Minister Grath at her favorite training spot in the open countryside just outside the Helkan capital.

"That news never fails to delight me," Grath quipped with a smile, wiping her face and neck with a towel. Tossing the towel to one of her household servants, she lowered her protective mask, twirled her combat swords and breathed deeply, preparing herself for the next sparring bout. "Go on, Raast. I can fight and listen at the same time." She squared off against her sparring partner, an agile young feme with whom she was now one bout for one. This last duel would settle a private wager between them. Grath moved first, an opening lunge. Her opponent parried. Grath twirled and swung, left sword, right, left again. She twirled and landed a backward kick to her opponent's midsection. The younger feme rolled with the blow, fell well, and sprung up in a fighting stance.

As Grath and her opponent breathed, facing off and circling each other for the next clash, Raast talked on. "She insists the presence of offworld mercenary forces on Zeln legally requires you to intervene on her behalf."

"I assume you've covered your tracks properly," Grath asked as she attacked again, her opponent blocking four thrusts and hopping over a sweeping kick.

"Naturally," Raast said with poorly concealed

irritation in her voice. Grath knew it annoyed her Chief of State whenever she even appeared to question her abilities. Not that she really needed to. But one must not allow one's staff to grow complacent, Grath reminded herself. Her opponent pressed in hard, twirling her swords with impressive speed. Grath barely managed to block all her thrusts as she retreated, waiting for an opening. "I made sure the money could never be traced back to you, of course. Nevertheless, Kelnaath has indisputable proof that offworld mercs fired on her forces as they attempted, quite legally, to retake nationalized territory which has never been recognized by the Council of Ministers. And, while she can't prove the money came from here, it's only a matter of time before she proves it didn't come from Zeln. She has a strong case. Legally, you are required to intervene."

Grath ducked a blade and gritted her teeth in pain as her opponent landed a knee to her gut. She took the pain and landed a blow to her opponent's mask with her left sword hilt, knocking her off balance. A desperate move, designed to buy time. "Don't worry," she said with false confidence, panting and circling her adversary. "The other ministers are always squeamish when it comes to military intervention. Unless Kelnaath can convincingly fake evidence of foreign involvement on Zeln, which I doubt, they won't be able to raise enough votes to force me to intervene."

"Not even with Combine money?"

Grath's opponent attacked, using the old Taarex gambit. Potent, but tiring. You had to finish your enemy off quickly for it to work. Grath parried, danced backward and stalled, saving her strength. "The one thing the Combines can't buy is courage," she gasped as her opponent picked up the pace and she struggled to keep up. "The inner worlds are distrustful of the

Council. They won't tolerate intervention, and the ministers know it." She made her move, using the old Braal gambit, spinning and slicing for the midsection. Her opponent avoided it, but it gave her the initiative.

"Kelnaath is generating rumors that Kaylenn is on Trynn, attempting illegal transactions with the Kaltaarists. Those rumors are already spreading to the inner planets. This could get ugly, especially if your promises of renewed agro trade aren't realized quickly."

Grath threw everything she had into her final gambit, a wild series of twirling attacks, confusing her enemy. She threw her off-balance, slipped in, got a leg behind her, and knocked her flat on her back, her sword against her throat. Her enemy dropped her swords, conceding Grath's victory. Grath helped her up, and they both removed their protective masks. Her face burning with exhaustion, Grath gulped greedily from the water glass her servant gave her, and studied the face of her vanquished opponent. A gorgeous young feme with black hair, slanted black eyes, strong cheek bones and a rich, gold-brown complexion. Beauty like that deserved to be won fairly, Grath told herself with pride, removing a glove and stroking a hand across the other feme's smiling, sweaty face, kissing her lightly on the lips. "My quarters, as agreed?" she whispered.

"As agreed," the other whispered with a smile.

Grath glanced at Raast, who looked very exasperated.

"Get Kaylenn back from Trynn as soon as possible. And get her to send me a time, cost and labor analysis of her proposed agricultural project. Make sure it's properly edited, of course, before I present it to the Council. Omit anything...compromising, regarding the Kaltaarists. Now, is there anything else?"

"Just one thing," Raast muttered as Grath climbed into her hovercar, accompanied by her newly won prize. "I know you said you didn't want to be disturbed about this, but Vaaltyr is becoming a problem."

"I thought I told you to jail her weeks ago!"

"I did, but the insurrection to free her is growing. There have been riots in the outer districts, and even in the capital itself. It's even beginning to spread offworld, to the other hub systems. This business on Zeln is helping to feed the anti-Kaltaarist propaganda."

"Well, torture her! Get her to make a public statement."

"I've tried. She won't break." Raast looked concerned. "I've never met anyone quite like her before."

Grath sighed in disgust. "I can't be bothered by this. Do what you have to do to maintain order. Invoke the Emergency Powers Clause if you must, but keep the streets clear of rabble! And send a few contingents to the offworld capitals, just to let the governors know I won't tolerate laxity. Do what you do best, Raast: invoke fear. Leave the Council with no doubt that I am in control."

"Yes, Prime Minister."

That nonsense out of the way, Grath turned her attention to more important matters. "Liquor?" she asked the lovely, vibrant young feme seated beside her.

Chapter 32

Timeline: Kalthaar Experiment
Timeline Spatial: Planet Trynn, in the galaxy of
Kalthaar
Timeline Chronological: The fourth millennium after
the age of Kaarth, section point 122959

"I could get used to the taste of this," Zaard remarked, savoring the flavor of the Velnyr Saaryth poured for her. *Delicate, this Kaltaarist wine, but intoxicating in a soft, pleasant sort of way. Disarming. Perhaps duplicitous, but quite irresistible.*

"In case you're interested," Saaryth whispered, leaning over her shoulder, "we do quite well exporting this stuff to the Kralite worlds. I'm told your merchant elite like to serve it at parties. It's considered exotic, conversational." She put her arms playfully around Zaard's neck. "Good for throwing bureaucrats and politicians off their guard."

Zaard pulled her across the white-padded divan on which she lounged and into her arms. It had been far too long, she realized as she kissed her. The war, first against the Vedrans, then against the Combines. The hate. No time ever for love. Love was weakness, so she had learned. She remembered the day the soldiers pulled her from her farm and drafted her into fuel shipping service. One stinking starship hold and filthy asteroid port after another. The war dragged on, and they transferred her to planetside combat duty. Dead worlds. Swamps and frozen wastes and deserts. They taught her to kill. She learned. She remembered the day she came home to learn most of her friends, and Trayl, a young feme she had loved, were dead. Killed risking their lives for a government that sold off their lands. Love was for fools. Or so she had thought.

Saaryth lay back in her lap and smiled up at her.

"Negotiations are proceeding well, I see," Kaylenn joked, stepping out of the sonic wave shower and pulling on a light robe.

"Jealous, love?" Saaryth teased, lifting a hand, invitingly. Kaylenn joined them on the divan, warm and eager for both of them. Zaard took great comfort in her, as she had these past weeks. Negotiations had dragged on, but once she had dropped her guard with Kaylenn and Saaryth, it was not a struggle anymore. More like a journey, closer and closer to what she had always wanted. Kaylenn was strong and intense against her. Not like Saaryth. Yet she loved them both. She had, long before she had accepted the wager of entering the hunt simulation with them. There were times when the jealousy still burned inside her. Days when she felt Saaryth would always own Kaylenn's heart, and perhaps her own as well. But when she held them both like this, jealousy vanished, and doubt with it.

The intercom buzzed shrilly, and Zaard cursed. "Let them go to—"

"It's a security override," Saaryth said, getting up off the divan and fastening the belt on her robe as she stepped over to the com terminal. "It's Zaalyn," she said, checking the call log. "She wouldn't disturb us unless it was urgent, rest assured."

Zaard groaned in frustration as she fastened her own robe and made herself look as dignified as possible. Kaylenn straightened the robe for her a bit, giving her hair a gentle stroke. Zaalyn's life-sized hologram image appeared in the center of the room. The First Planner looked even more dour and serious than usual, and was dressed in her ritual blue robe.

"I apologize for this intrusion," she said icily, and perhaps with an uncharacteristic hint of fear in her voice. "Word has just come to me from my people on Zeln. Earlier today, Zed-4 came under attack by military forces of Zeln's Southern Continental Province, supported by the Army of the Planetary Governor."

Zaard's old hatred came welling up in her stomach, her teeth clenching. If she had not been here wasting her time. She looked at Kaylenn. She had trusted her. Kaylenn closed her eyes, then opened them again.

"How well did our side do?" she asked.

Zaalyn sighed, columns of figures scrolling up on the air beside her. "The details are coming through now. There should be a printout reaching you now as well." Saaryth pulled sheets out of the printer and quickly glanced through them, handing sheets to Kaylenn. "In summation: The invading force was destroyed by the Zed-4 militia, supported by the army of the Provincial Governor General, and apparently offworld mercenaries."

Kaylenn offered Zaard a printed sheet and she snatched it from her hand. Although the casualties among her people were high, she was oddly relieved to note they were nowhere near as high as would have been expected when the Transtar Combine had still controlled Zed-4. She noticed the casualty figures of Kaylenn's people were quite heavy. Even the force commander, Kolis, had sustained severe battlefield injury and was in hospital. She looked at Kaylenn again, feeling somewhat guilty for having doubted her loyalty. "Has Kelnaath made an official statement?" Kaylenn asked with the cold calm of a military commander.

"Yes," Zaalyn replied. "She has declared the Northern Continental Province an outlaw state and has called upon the other five provinces of Zeln to join her in suppressing the rebellion. So far, only the Southern

Province has responded."

"Those wolves would take any excuse to seize our lands," Kaylenn grumbled under her breath.

"The governors of the remaining four provinces are still negotiating with the Planetary Governor, but according to my sources, they are all leaning toward Kelnaath's position."

Kaylenn sighed, crumpling a sheet of paper and ripping it in half. "Kelnaath is bolder than I gave her credit for, the snake. I didn't expect her to move this soon."

"We have to go back!" Zaard said in desperation, clutching Kaylenn's arm.

"We will, of course," Kaylenn said supportively, taking Zaard's hand in hers. Saaryth put her hands on both of theirs. "First Planner..." Kaylenn began, looking at the hologram.

"Your transportation back to Zeln has already been arranged. However..." she looked hesitant. "Be advised, Kelnaath has called for the executions of all three of you. I understand your need to command your forces on Zeln, but it might be more prudent to command from a safer location, outside the Zeln system."

"I owe it to my people to fight beside them," Zaard declared in anger. Kaylenn and Saaryth embraced her. "I can't rally my troops from offworld!"

"Trynn can't be moved to a safer location if we lose this fight," Saaryth pointed out. Zaalyn looked frightened at the implication.

"Let me go back, alone," Kaylenn said. Zaard looked at her in shock. "This is between Kelnaath and me. I gave you my word I'd handle her, Zaard," she said softly. "I'll keep that promise."

Zaard pulled Kaylenn against her and held her tightly. Saaryth held them both.

Chapter 33

Timeline: Kalthaar Experiment
Timeline Spatial: Office of the Planetary Governor,
Planet Zeln, in the galaxy of Kalthaar
Timeline Chronological: The fourth millennium after
the age of Kaarth, section point 122960

Kelnaath sipped her coffee and smiled. "I knew Daalkri would come onboard," she gloated to Kyrr, her Lieutenant Governor. "With the Southern and Eastern continents pressing Kaylenn between them, it's only a matter of days before the two polar provinces commit troops."

"That still leaves the western islands," Kyrr put in with a cautionary tone.

"Insignificant," Kelnaath said with a dismissive wave of her hand. "The worst they'll do is stay neutral. Their army is the smallest of the six anyway."

"Still, we need their bases," the tall, blonde feme pointed out, calling Kelnaath's attention to the globe of Zeln on her desk. "Otherwise, supply lines could become a problem."

"Don't worry so much, Kyrr," she said with a smile, running a hand affectionately along Kyrr's well-muscled arm. "Coryn will come around soon enough. She doesn't dare defy the Combines any more than the other governors do. All they have to do is move a few of their factories offworld, and any governor who crosses them will find herself facing angry, unemployed mobs." She laughed, patting Kyrr's arm. "Besides, the tide of public opinion is with us right now. Anti-Kaltaarist sentiment is growing, here and in the hub systems. Kaylenn and her rebel allies will be dealt with soon enough. Once the Northern Continent has been carved up and sold off to the highest bidders...then I'll move on Trynn." The thought of that delighted her.

She felt Kyrr pulling away. She looked at her, and her trusted friend looked concerned. "Would Prime Minister Grath approve of—"

"To the Void with Grath! The Combines have made it clear she's an obstacle that must be removed. Trynn is another annoyance they want eliminated. The Kaltaarists and their perverted little terraforming projects give people ideas we can do without in our society. I'll make an example of Trynn, and that will earn me the gratitude of the Combines, as well as the praise of the Kaltie-haters on Helkos. Their power base is growing, largely due to Combine support." She drummed her fingers together and smiled, hungrily. "Who knows? If I time this right, someday the office of the Prime Minister might just be mi--"

The intercom buzzed, interrupting her train of thought. She opened the channel. "What is it?!"

"A message from offworld, Governor," her secretary said. "It's from Kaylenn, Governor General of-"

"Of nothing!" Kelnaath interrupted. "Is she calling to surrender?" She licked her lips, anticipating victory.

"No, Governor. She is calling to challenge you to the Great Hunt. She invokes the Primary Law, and demands you meet her at a time and place to be assigned by the Helkan Council of Ministers. To face her and eight other champions of the Zeln provinces, also to be appointed by the Helkan Council, in the hunt for the daughter of Kral. For the governorship of Zeln. Shall I transmit a reply? Governor? Governor, are you there?" Kelnaath roared in rage as she smashed the intercom with her coffee mug, electrical sparks flying from the shorted circuits.

Chapter 34

"So cold..." Faln murmured, slipping in and out of time-shift.

Ralyn held her daughter against her, covering her with her cloak. The child's teeth chattered, as though she were immersed in ice. "What is it, Faln," she said with concern, kissing the child's forehead. "Where are you?"

"Ice and snow everywhere," she muttered, her voice trembling. "The wind...it screams." She trembled in fear. "Something's coming closer..."

Chapter 35

Timeline: Kalthaar Experiment
Timeline Spatial: Just outside the planetary system of Planet Zeln, in the galaxy of Kalthaar
Timeline Chronological: The fourth millennium after the age of Kaarth, section point 123117

Saaryth fastened her jacket tightly, the cold shipboard air chilling her to her bones as she stepped off the lift onto the lowermost deck of the starship. She walked down the poorly lit passageway, and quickened her pace as she heard the sounds of combat coming from the chamber ahead.

She found Kaylenn and Zaard squaring off against each other with fighting staffs. They had been at it a while, and had worked up quite a sweat. Saaryth folded her arms and leaned against a bulkhead, watching the match. They were both in good form, physically. Though, perhaps both a bit too angry for their own good. She could see it in the hot red exertion of their faces. They gave it a rest, finally, each leaning forward onto her knees and gasping, their breath white and steaming in the frosty air. "We're entering the Zeln system," Saaryth said dryly.

Kaylenn jogged in place for a moment, then stepped over to a water spigot and wet a towel, mopping her face. She wet another towel and handed it to Zaard.

"Any last minute surprises?" she asked, breathless.

"No," Saaryth sighed. "Protests are still flying from Kelnaath and the other provincial governors, but Grath seems to be holding firm on the present selection. The two of you will face Kelnaath and the other seven whose computer bios you've already studied." She looked at both of them with exasperation. "Unless, of course..."

"No government in exile for me, Saaryth," Zaard said firmly. "Convey my apologies to Zaalyn."

"We'll be all right, love," Kaylenn said reassuringly, draping the towel about her neck, and extending her hand invitingly to Saaryth. "The others are good, but quite ordinary. Grath clearly made the selections in our favor. She has too much invested in us not to. I've studied Kelnaath. She's the best of the lot, but between the two of us, Zaard and I should handle her easily. She's an assassin, not a warrior."

"She's the best at what she does," Saaryth said with some irritation at Kaylenn's bravado. She did not appreciate being shielded. "Fifteen missions behind Vedran lines and, unlike us, she never got caught."

"Unlike us, she was never betrayed," Kaylenn said with a smile, taking Saaryth's hand and kissing her on the cheek.

"She slipped through their best security systems, destroyed a number of their installations, and assassinated several of their high-ranking fleet commanders. She's never failed."

"First time for everything," Zaard said impudently, her strong arm slipping around Saaryth's waist. "Feel my strength?" she whispered playfully, kissing her.

Saaryth sighed in frustration, kissing both of them. "I know you both think I'm weak. I should be giving this venture my wholehearted support. In my mind, I know it's the best chance we have of saving both our worlds. But, in my heart... I can't face the thought of losing you both." They both embraced her, gently and comfortingly. Saaryth made her move, kneeing Kaylenn sharply in the gut. As she gasped and doubled over, Saaryth caught Zaard off-guard with an upward blow to her chin followed by a chop to the nerve in her neck. As

Zaard dropped to the floor, stunned, Saaryth kicked Kaylenn's legs out from under her. As she went down, Saaryth pulled the six-inch blade from her jacket sleeve, pulled Kaylenn by her hair to a kneeling position in front of her, and pressed the blade's edge to her carotid artery. "If that had been for real, you'd both be dead now." Zaard struggled to get up, rubbing her neck and looking angry. "Two Kralites, tricked by a Kaltaarist! How well do you expect to do against a professional assassin?"

She took the blade from Kaylenn's throat and helped her to her feet. Kaylenn slapped her and grabbed the knife from her hand.

"What was that supposed to prove?" she hissed.

"It's not as though we trust Kelnaath," Zaard barked, shoving Saaryth roughly.

"She doesn't need your trust!" Saaryth shouted, dropping all pretense and letting her anger flow. "All she needs is one moment of carelessness!"

Chapter 36

Timeline: Kalthaar Experiment
Timeline Spatial: Planet Helkos, in the galaxy of Kalthaar
Timeline Chronological: The fourth millennium after the age of Kaarth, section point 123117

If there was one thing Grath hated more than council assemblies with her conniving, back-stabbing ministers, it was those rare, excruciating moments when she had to deal with clergy. The High Priestess of her tribe's matron goddess, accompanied by her staff and retainers, was given the full honors, of course. Including a full military escort into the capital, the most famous singer in the Helkos Confederation accompanied by a full chorus, singing the ballad of the blessed Kaarth in the largest concert hall on the planet, before a live audience of thousands. Grath hated the pomp and circumstance, but Raast had insisted it was essential for her public image right now.

Grath received the dour-faced old priestess in the diplomatic office normally reserved for foreign ambassadors. Grath's favorite painting, a classical nude by the great Kalthaaran artist Quayne had been removed at Rasst's suggestion, along with every piece of fine sculpture that might be deemed offensive, and replaced by a traditional motif of the goddesses fighting Kral. Grath hated it. She had never had any use for the old school of religious art. The old priestess sat in the wide-backed, black-upholstered armchair facing Grath, her brightly-colored silken robes, jeweled veils and gold adornments making her look like one of the goddess-queens of legend. Her acolyte, an attractive young feme in traditional maroon robes, handed her an incense pipe and lit it for her with a laser torch. Raast stood by in full military dress uniform complete with gold piping. She looked more decorated than Grath. Grath fought to maintain a smile. "I trust you are enjoying your stay in the capital, your eminence."

"Let us dispense with pleasantries, Prime Minister," the crone said with cold disdain, her piercing black eyes fixed on Grath's. "I am here, representing not only the temple of the Holy Kaarth, but the entire Pantheon of Priestesses. Your policy regarding the Zeln situation is not only in brazen violation of the Primary Law, it is a blasphemy against four thousand years of sacred tradition! It is an affront to the spiritual values of Helkan society, to every goddess, and to the spirit of Kral Herself. What have you to say?"

She played it cool, trying to appear respectful, while wanting desperately to show her contempt for the pious old hypocrite. "I'm afraid I'm a bit confused, Eminence. Primary Law was invoked by Kaylenn of Zeln, and Primary Law demands that Kelnaath, the present Governor of Zeln, answer. Her position as leader of her empire has been challenged in the name of Kral, and like the goddess-queens of your... our sacred texts, she is required to respond and submit herself to Kral's judgment. In fact, and I say this with the utmost respect, for as long as I can remember, the Pantheon of Priestesses has complained that Helkan society was slipping further and further away from tradition, that we have grown lax in allowing our leaders to come to power through politics rather than by winning their positions on the hunt as did the goddess-queens of antiquity. You have complained that we've permitted the hunt to become merely ceremonial, allowing it to decide only minor administrative positions over nothing larger than a production sector. Well, this hunt will decide the governorship of an entire planet! The entire Confederation is talking about it. How have I erred in this matter?"

"Not one of the ten hunters of this gathering was approved by the Pantheon, Prime Minister, as you very well know! For the selection to be made by a secular political head such as yourself, rather than by the Priestesses of Kral-"

"Forgive me." Grath interrupted. Raast strained desperately, obviously anguished at Grath having interrupted the priestess mid-sentence. Grath fought to repress a smirk. "I was under the impression that tradition demanded the tribal leader make the selection. In the context of contemporary society, does that not mean me?"

The priestess's eyes widened with shock. "You dare compare yourself with the goddess-queens? With the divine mothers of our orders?"

"Your Eminence, I meant no disrespect, but I myself was the product of a fine gathering, all ten hunters, my mother included, selected by the Pantheon."

"But you yourself have never participated in a hunt, Prime Minister. Your position in this office has never been officially recognized by the Pantheon or, for that matter, by the order of Kaarth."

Perhaps because I haven't been as generous to the Pantheon as my Combine-controlled predecessors, she thought bitterly. "Yes, well nevertheless, Primary Law and Kalthaaran tradition state that, unless you can find some specific reason why any of these hunters are ineligible to participate, supported by the sacred texts, the decision of the tribal leader—myself—stands."

"There is such a reason, Prime Minister! A very obvious reason! Primary Law states that each of the ten must fight alone. No groups are allowed to collaborate in fighting Kral. Each of the ten is judged by Her alone! It is common knowledge that this Kaylenn has formed a political alliance with Zaard, another of the ten you selected. The two of them are partners in this new government which I believe is in dispute, are they not? In addition, it has been brought to my attention that both of them were recently in residence on that abominable planet, Trynn." She said the name with revulsion, circling her incense pipe in a ritualistic gesture to ward off evil. "A Kaltaarist world. It has been indicated to me that they have been involved in covert, possibly illegal, probably heretical negotiations with the witches of that cursed planet! I have also heard disturbing rumors that the two of them may have been involved in a perverse trinary relationship with a Kaltaarist named Saaryth! All of this would render Kaylenn and Zaard ineligible on numerous grounds, not the least of which is collusion! They are clearly allies, if not lovers."

"First, Eminence, while there have been political and/or diplomatic contacts between Kaylenn, a provincial governor, and Zaard, the administrator of one of several production sectors in Kaylenn's province, it is far from established that they are allies, much less partners in anything resembling a 'new government.'" She smiled slightly. "As to what trade negotiations might have taken place on Trynn, it is not at all unusual for a provincial governor to be accompanied by one or more of her production administrators on such diplomatic missions. To the best of my knowledge, the negotiations were confined to interstellar commerce, and did at no time enter the realm of the covert, the illegal, or the heretical. As to any idle rumors of...illicit intimacy, well..." she bowed her head, feigning embarrassment. "There will always be such rumors. Idle gossip is a vice of our times, as

I've heard Your Eminence say at numerous services. I have learned to ignore such innuendo. However, even assuming for the sake of argument that Kaylenn and Zaard are allies of one sort or another... does this necessarily violate tradition?"

"Of course it does!"

"Does it? Even for our order? After all, weren't Kaarth and Jaeven lovers?"

The priestess's face blanched. Raast appeared on the verge of rupturing a blood vessel. Grath was actually beginning to enjoy this meeting. "You blaspheme!" the priestess cried. "Kaarth redeemed herself in the eyes of Kral by slaying the faithless Jaeven who led her into sin and then tried to tempt her into the camp of Kaltaari!"

"Yes. Then Kaarth was later killed by her daughter, Braal. I've often wondered about that. If Kaarth had done things the way Jaeven wanted, both would have lived. Because she didn't, they both died. Odd, don't you think?"

One last ritual twirl of the pipe, a bit of ground crystal tossed onto the carpeting, and the priestess rose stiffly from her chair. "I hereby declare you excommunicated!" she said in rage, pointing her finger at Grath. "The entire Pantheon shall condemn you for this heresy! Publicly."

"Eminence, please," Raast said in desperation, approaching the priestess with a respectful bow. "I'm sure the Prime Minister meant no insult."

"Certainly not," Grath said pleasantly, rising from her chair. "I merely engaged in a bit of harmless speculation. At any rate, I simply meant that we should give Kaylenn and Zaard the benefit of the doubt. Once the hunt is on, and they're both out in the wilds fighting for their survival, one of them might do the right thing and stab the other in the back."

Looking shocked, the priestess tossed her veil across her face and departed in a huff, her acolyte and attendants following. Raast stood with mouth agape, staring at Grath.

"Well. I'm glad that's over. I desperately need a drink. Care to join me?"

"What did you think you were doing?" Raast demanded in an onraged whisper. "Insulting the High Priestess of your own order! This is just the sort of thing the opposition parties jump on in times like these! Short of claiming temporary insanity, how do you expect me to explain this to the council?"

"The old hag would have excommunicated me anyway! She came here to give me one last chance to surrender Zeln to the Combines, and I wasn't about to do that. Don't you understand, Raast? The Pantheon is as much owned by the Combines as most of the ministers are. There are a few among the ministers who perhaps have the courage to stand up to the Combines, but only if I lead the way. So, by inviting the public condemnation of the Pantheon—"

"You raise your flag, and see who salutes?"

"You're learning, Raast. Now, about that drink?"

"Thank you, no," she said, tight-lipped. "I think one of us should stay sober."

Grath sneered at her. "Suit yourself. Get someone to put the paintings and statuary back the way they were, will you? Oh, and while you're at it...get that garbage picked up off the carpet," she said, pointing at the ground blue crystals the priestess had thrown.

"I'll see to it. But, before you have that drink, Prime Minister..."

"Yes?"

"I think you should know the Pantheon's displeasure will only exacerbate a worsening situation."

"Meaning?"

"The situation with Vaaltyr."

Grath kicked a chair in disgust. "I thought I told you—"

"I did as you said, but mobs in the streets aren't the problem anymore. It's work stoppages. Entire production sectors are shutting down in protest. It's spreading through a dozen worlds, and this scandal with Kaylenn is making it worse by the day. The Pantheon is calling the stoppage 'abstention from work and fasting,' but our offworld creditors are calling it something else."

"Vaaltyr is the rallying point? Make her disappear."

"The last thing we need now is a martyr!"

"Did I say to kill her? I said, 'make her disappear!' Press her into offworld labor. Ship her off to some remote mining colony, in the company of the countless petty thieves and layabouts we ship out there every week. Lose her in the system. They can't protest for her release if no one remembers where she is! In fact, drop the criminal charges and find a way to get her into indentured service. No one protests over the fate of some loser in debtor service. Just make her fade away. They'll forget about her."

"Until someone else comes along."

Chapter 37

Timeline: Kalthaar Experiment
Timeline Spatial: Planet Zeln, in the galaxy of Kalthaar
*Timeline Chronological: The fourth millennium after
the age of Kaarth, section point 123119*

Kelnaath turned, silently and gracefully, the biting cold embracing her like the skintight bodysuit she wore. The wind screamed over the icy wastes. She closed her eyes and focused, finding her center. Somewhere, beyond the wind, was the enemy. Both enemies. Sapien and Beast. Her instincts told her the moment was close. Waiting. Waiting. There. A footstep crunching in the snow. Wait. Crouch. Become one with the storm and the snow. The enemy came within her reach. She opened her eyes and sprang. She clenched her fists, and the twin blades strapped to her forearms extended simultaneously. The other feme looked up, and her finger tightened on the trigger of her harpoon rifle. Kelnaath dropped to avoid the flying harpoon, and sliced cleanly through her opponent's gut. She sprang up to a standing position, and the second blade cut straight up, through the other feme's throat and slid into her brain.

She had just retracted the blades and picked up the rifle when she heard the sound of Kral's deadly claws scratching against the ice. A sharp beeping in her headset made her curse. She pressed the contact at her belt, triggering the auto shut-down of the computer simulation. The sensory illusion of ice and snowfields and blizzard vanished, and she found herself surrounded by the gray steel walls of her training chamber. Kyrr stood before her, shivering in the cold, her breath steaming.

"What is it, Kyrr?" Kelnaath asked, disconnecting

the sensory contact patches and attached wires from her head, arms and legs.

"It's 04:20, Governor," Kyrr said. "You told me to notify you."

"Any word from Helkos? Has old Grath changed her mind?" A part of her desperately hoped the answer would be 'no.'

"I'm afraid she has not, Governor." Her old friend looked concerned. "I've transmitted signed letters of protest from all five provincial governors, invoked every relevant clause of the Home Rule Provision of the Confederation Charter, but she won't budge. She insists, in the interest of impartiality, the selections must be made-"

Kelnaath held up a hand. "Spare me her rationalizations. We both know what she wants. I'll enjoy taking her down along with Kaylenn!"

Kyrr approached her, a worried look in her aqua-blue eyes. "Governor... Kelnaath." She let the barriers of protocol slip. "I do not doubt your abilities, but the reports say that Kaylenn and Zaard are both formidable. The risk is unnecessary. I ask you again, please refuse the challenge."

"And give Grath an excuse to remove me from office for violating Primary Law? Never!"

"Primary Law hasn't been invoked to oust a government official in-"

"It's not about legalities, old friend. It's about politics. Grath has her own agenda. Besides, I can't appear weak in the eyes of the Combines, or make it difficult for the Pantheon to endorse me. This is a moment in history, my friend," she said, laying a hand on Kyrr's shoulder. "No time for retreat or caution. This is my one and only chance to eliminate all my rivals at once. I can handle Kaylenn and Zaard."

"And Kral? Everyone says this version of Her is the

most lethal ever."

"I've studied it thoroughly, and it's within my ability. Don't worry." She clasped her by the shoulders. "I know I can trust and depend on you to fill the governor's chair and keep my powerbase secure against my enemies while I'm gone." The corners of Kyrr's mouth turned up ever so slightly for a second, her eyes momentarily flashing with ambition. Kelnaath reached behind Kyrr's head and unfastened her hair, letting it fall in gold tresses over her broad shoulders. "It's been far too long since we've been this close...and undistracted by work, old friend." She kissed Kyrr on the lips, slipping her tongue into her lover's mouth as she unfastened Kyrr's uniform jacket.

"It's cold here," Kyrr protested.

"I'll keep you warm." She laughed softly as she pressed her body against Kyrr's firm, well-developed frame. "I'll be facing death soon. I've trained as much as I dare. I want to spend this last day with you. Embracing life. Kiss me." Kyrr complied. Kelnaath slipped her hand inside the other feme's shirt and felt her way up her muscular chest to her breasts. As fine as she had remembered them. She heard Kyrr gasp as she clenched her fist and drove one of the blades through her subordinate's heart. Kelnaath smiled and kissed her one last time as the look of pained shock slipped from Kyrr's comely face, replaced by resignation. Kelnaath slid the blade out of her chest, and Tyrr's large bulk fell to the floor, dead, at her feet. Kelnaath smiled as she licked warm blood from the blade, even as it steamed in the chill air. "All my rivals at once," she whispered in delight. "You're next, Kaylenn."

Chapter 38

Timeline: Kalthaar Experiment
Timeline Spatial: Planet Zeln, in the galaxy of Kalthaar
Timeline Chronological: The fourth millennium after
the age of Kaarth, section point 123120

Kaylenn clasped Saaryth's hand as she turned to step onto the transport shuttle. Though it may have violated both propriety and politics, she could not resist embracing and kissing Saaryth one last time. She took her by the shoulders and looked at her, savoring her. Her beauty, her sheer love, undimmed since that day at the spaceport on Helkos so long ago. "Come back to me," Saaryth whispered, leaning close by her ear. "Both of you."

"I love you," Kaylenn whispered as she turned and jogged up the boarding ramp into the hold of the transport. The other nine were already assembled, seated in two rows facing each other across the hold. She looked them over as they sat there in their white thermal suits and snow gear. Hard femes. Soldiers, like herself. Once. Resigned expressions on most of them. Little more than draftees serving the orders of their governors. Supposedly 'defending the honor of their clusters,' or 'representing their provinces.' In reality, risking death in an archaic ritual to serve the murky designs of politicians and corporations. Kaylenn began to hate herself for what she was doing to them. They were innocent in all this.

A few had hungry, envious looks of ambition in their eyes. Common soldiers given a chance for real power for the first time in their lives, dropped into their hands like a gift from the goddesses. Poor, naive fools. Most of them would not stand a chance against Kelnaath, let alone Kral. Foregoing the traditions of old, neither Kaylenn nor Zaard had been required to lay with any of them in the traditional preparation for the Great Hunt, for which Kaylenn was very grateful. She remembered stories of the dark, musky chambers of legend, where the chosen ten engaged in group copulation until, at the climax of their passion, the huzzing, flittering life-givers would taste their blood, combine it with that of the preceding princess daughter and pass it on to Kral. Then, the ten would sleep in a circle near Kral's nest until the monster Kaaldrin that would become Her took the precious jewel from each of them and combined all ten into the next daughter that would rule the empire. All that had been replaced by the cold, antiseptic extraction of blood samples in sterile laboratories.

Her eyes met Zaard's. They couldn't afford to let the others notice, not even for a moment. They looked away, and Kaylenn seated herself in the row opposite Zaard, staring straight ahead at the gray steel bulkhead. She heard the soft whir of hydraulics as the boarding ramp rose and the hatch sealed with a clank. "Rumor has it she's yours," the feme seated beside her whispered in her ear. She turned sharply and found herself facing Kelnaath's handsome face, her dark eyes sparkling cruelly, her smile wicked. "I'll make sure you get to watch her die."

"Before or after I cut out your liver and eat it, witch?" Kaylenn whispered through clenched teeth.

"Brave talk from a commander who lost an entire ship and crew." She smiled broadly. Kaylenn refused to give her the satisfaction of showing anger. "Tell me, how is the Kaltaarist in bed, eh? Shall I make her my little pet once I've brought her your head on my spear?" Kaylenn's fist tightened on the hilt of her knife just as the lift rockets engaged and the hold shook around her.

"'Saaryth,' is it?" She giggled sadistically as the air shuttle lifted from its hangar bay and jetted into open sky. "I'm told she looks a little like me. The goddesses and their renowned sense of irony, eh? I'm curious to see how well she serves my pleasure, and how creatively, before I slit her pretty throat."

Kaylenn took a deep breath and forced herself to relax, as Saaryth had taught her. *Forget the shadows.* She had to stay in control. Her life depended on it. She smiled. "You do look a bit like her, at that. Though, not nearly as pleasing to the eye. Still, you've given me a good idea. What say, after I've cut off all four of your limbs, I take my pleasure from you? You can show me what whore's tricks you know. You must have a hundred of them to have survived as long as you have. Amuse me, and I might reward you with a swift, easy death. Bore me, and I'll gut you from the inside out." One last, contemptuous sneer, and Kelnaath looked away. Kaylenn permitted herself one glance at Zaard's smiling face.

An hour later, the air shuttle neared the place of the great hunt. "Your turn, Kaylenn," the Helkan observer shouted over the screaming wind, the airborne shuttle's hold open to the freezing polar air as the boarding hatch was opened.

Kaylenn adjusted her goggles and breathing filter, unstrapped from her flight harness and stepped in front of the hatch. The wind cut through her thermal suit like a laser, the folds of her hood and jacket rattling noisily. She looked down at the barren, gleaming white expanse of Zeln's northern polar ice cap. One of the few pristine lands left in her world. Glacial. Wild. Untamed. A place whose natural rigors made it a training ground for soldiers and a place for the younger, sturdier femes of the 'leisure classes' to explore and find adventure. Some found death.

"Now!" the observer shouted.

Kaylenn made the jump. Kelnaath's voice cried out on the wind: "Be seeing you, Kaylenn!" The wind blasted through her as she fell spreadeagled on the icy air, the ice cliffs hurtling up at her. The glowing red numerals of the holochronometer in her goggles clicked off the seconds. When it hit 0:00, she pressed the button on her harness, and her chute opened, yanking her roughly upright. The parachute spreading wide, the wind carried her north over the frozen sea, toward the snowfields in the deep valley between the mountains beyond.

She braced for the drop. Faster and faster rose the white ground. She groaned in pain as she struck ground, tucking and rolling in the half-frozen snow. The chute tangled and flapped fiercely in the wind. She unlocked the harness and slipped out, leaving the chute to drift free across the ice sheet.

The radio tracker strapped to her wrist pointed her toward the beacon attached to the supply drop they would be making now. Her weapons, shelter and provisions came down about a hundred feet from her drop site, the chute fluttering down as she ran to it in the deep snow. She tore open the package and slung on the enclosed belts and rifle. Surveying the frozen landscape, she pulled the holoviewer from her beltpack and put it to her goggles, checking the map. Judging by the terrain and its proximity to the sea, she was about twelve klicks south of the Heltryth Ice Flow. Zaard's drop had been roughly twenty klicks to the northeast, so with luck, they should meet up at the third signal marker from Kaylenn's present position.

She inventoried the equipment she had been allowed: One harpoon rifle with six steel-tipped harpoons, one steel-tipped spear, a hand ax, climbing gear, inflatable tent, medikit, small portable heating unit with maybe three days worth in the power cell, three emergency heating flares, three days field rations (barely), compass, and snow shoes. She strapped on the shoes, slung on the heavy pack and set off into the swirling snows.

Chapter 39

Timeline: Kalthaar Experiment
Timeline Spatial: Near the Heltryth Ice Flow, Planet Zeln, in the galaxy of Kalthaar
Timeline Chronological: The fourth millennium after the age of Kaarth, section point 123120

Her heart beat hot in a body turning quickly to ice as she approached the third signal marker, a tantalizing black shadow and a flashing red light amid the white blur of wind-blown snow ahead. Zaard would be in her arms soon. The two of them in a warm tent beside two heating units. She quickened her pace, shaking off another damned layer of snow. She wiped the icy buildup from her goggles, trying to see the signal marker clearly. It seemed half buried, a mound of snow accumulated at its base. Her heart froze as she realized there was a body slumped against it.

She ran, pleading to whatever goddess would listen. She stopped in her tracks, cursing herself for a fool. Such obvious bait. She unslung her harpoon rifle, adjusted her goggles and scanned the surrounding terrain with radar imaging. Nothing appeared in the snow drifts that did not belong there. What about under the snow? She opened her pack and extracted an ice piton. She hurled it, watching through the sites of her rifle as it spun toward the corpse, landing several yards away. Nothing moved. Just the wind. On the wind she caught scents that reminded her of the war, the smells of a bad death, strong enough to discern through her respirator mask. She approached cautiously, her finger tight on the rifle's trigger.

She reached the body and dug, almost afraid to uncover it. It lay there, face down in the snow, the head covered by hood and goggles. She paused a moment and closed her eyes, remembering Zaard as she had been, on Trynn. On the hunt sim. In her quarters, with Saaryth. The warmth of her lips, and the sweet taste of wine. She opened her eyes, and pulled the body onto its back. The stiff, frozen features of a stranger stared up at her. She bowed her head and exhaled, filled with relief.

Brushing aside more snow, she saw the feme's lower torso had been partially devoured. Kral had lain in wait near the signal marker, knowing someone would come, eventually. Kaylenn reminded herself this was probably Kral's most lethal incarnation. Bred for the glacial clime, swift and cunning, possessing fifty percent more ganglia than the earlier variants, this one had race memory. Written into its genes was the accumulated experience of earlier hunts, passed on through the blood of sapien victors. Her mother's blood, and her own, included. Its instincts were far more acute and vicious than those of the old jungle-dwelling Kalthaaran breed. This one did not just defend itself against sapiens; it hunted them.

She searched the body of the dead feme, looking for identification. She found it. The nameplate on her tunic read: Jeltryn, West Sea Island Province. Kaylenn sighed at the damned, wasteful stupidity of all this. The western islands had no designs on the northern continent, or any other province on Zeln. They had just wanted to be left alone. But, politics had demanded they send a warrior to represent them in the Great Hunt. *Young. Probably never even seen combat.*

Kaylenn touched the signal beacon, savoring the warmth rising from its power coil. She removed one glove and placed her hand against the machine's scanning plate. The machine hummed. "I.D. confirmed", the flat, mechanical voice spat out. "Kaylenn, north continental province. Third signal.

Status: alive." She lifted Jeltryn's one remaining hand, and placed it against the scanner. "I.D. confirmed. Jeltryn, west sea island province. Fifth signal. Status: dead."

Kaylenn took Jeltryn's supply of harpoons and added them to her own arsenal. She stared off into the trackless snow. Why had Zaard not met her? If Kral had headed east after killing Jeltryn, Zaard might have crossed Her path. Her hand tightened on her rifle. She checked her compass, and set off east.

Chapter 40

Timeline: Kalthaar Experiment
Timeline Spatial: Governor General's headquarters,
Planet Zeln, in the galaxy of Kalthaar
Timeline Chronological: The fourth millennium after
the age of Kaarth, section point 123120

At the Governor General's headquarters on Zeln's North Continent, the progress of the Hunt was being closely followed. "One hunter confirmed dead, one more unaccounted for," Saaryth read from her computer terminal, now linked directly into the satellite tracking system monitoring the hunt. "Kaylenn registered about two minutes ago." The relief was visible in her voice.

"What about Zaard?" Zelkys asked anxiously.

"She last registered... twenty-eight minutes ago." Her hand clenched in concern. She took care not to let Zelkys or Kolis see it. "That put her about five klicks from Kaylenn's position."

"They should have linked up by now," Zelkys said with worry. Kolis laid a strong, comforting hand on her shoulder.

"Perhaps they have," Saaryth said, trying to allay her own fear more than that of the others. "Remember, they have to maintain the illusion of being competitors on this hunt. Zaard wouldn't have dared register at the same signal beacon, just moments after Kaylenn."

"She's right, Zelkys," Kolis said with uncharacteristic gentleness in her voice. "Besides, you know your Zaard is a fine warrior. She gave Kelnaath no end of grief here in Zed-4, and she'll cut her to pieces in the snow just as well."

"I know," Zelkys muttered, putting her hand on Kolis's. "I know she can't beat Zaard. But, Kral..."

"I've seen Zaard fight that devil," Saaryth said. "In her mind, where every battle is won or lost. Zaard won, with Kaylenn's help. They'll win again."

"Come on, Zelkys," Kolis said in a soft tone, bending over Zelkys's chair. "We, uh, should probably inspect the guard posts along the perimeter, just in case the acting planetary governor gets bold." She glanced up nervously at Saaryth. Such an obvious excuse for them to be alone. Kelnaath had left no one alive in her office with the daring or ambition to seize power in her absence, and Kolis knew it.

Zelkys smiled slightly and laid a hand affectionately on Kolis's broad arm as she accompanied her out of the room, apparently less concerned about appearances than Kolis. Saaryth could not stifle a grin, just a bit. She knew exactly how Zelkys felt. Zelkys turned at the door and looked at her. "You will notify us immediately, if…"

"Of course," Saaryth said, not looking up at her. A sharp, irritating buzz sounded in her ear, followed by Zaalyn's cold voice.

Report, Saaryth. Cursing under her breath, she translated all data on the hunt into encrypted sequence and uploaded it through her private com-channel into the offworld com satellite. The hyperspace transmission would reach Trynn within minutes. She pulled the micro receiver from her ear and slammed it angrily onto the desk.

As she buried her face in her hands, the words of her village priestess haunted her mind. *Forget the shadows. Remember the light. The individual is a fleeting shadow. Kaltaari is the eternal light. Do not grieve for those you have lost. They have become one with the Eternal. To grieve for them is vanity. Succumb to that temptation, and you will be as a shadow before the all-consuming light.* She clenched her fists and cried. What a bitter joke that two daughters of Kral would embrace the meaning of those words with so much more courage than she.

Chapter 41

Timeline: Kalthaar Experiment
Timeline Spatial: Near the Heltryth Ice Flow, Planet
Zeln, in the galaxy of Kalthaar
Timeline Chronological: The fourth millennium after
the age of Kaarth, section point 123120

Kaylenn found two more of the hunters dead upon reaching the ice flow. Kral had scattered chewed bits of them across the ice. Zaard was not one of them. Kaylenn gritted her teeth hatefully, the damnable snow rising in a swirling storm, the howling wind mocking her.

Forcing herself to concentrate, she surveyed the area. Not all of the blood frozen into the snow was sapien. Judging by the hard, crystallized black patches here and there, it was obvious at least one of the hunters had wounded Kral before dying. She followed the trail toward the northern tip of the flow, all the while scanning with radar.

Kaylenn's radar scan detected something moving up ahead, not yet visible through the drifting snows. *Definitely not sapien, by its shape.* Her heart racing, she prepared her harpoon rifle and circled in on her quarry, which seemed to be staying put. Feeding on its prey, perhaps. She moved in, scanning the surrounding hills with infrared first, just to make sure no sapien enemy might choose to pick her off with a clean shot rather than fight her for the prize after Kral was dead. Nothing warm registered out there in the ice and snow.

She turned back to her quarry, her heart pounding in anticipation. Then she stopped, surprised to see the shimmering red ghost of a warm-blooded animal registering on her scanner. *Kral's body temperature shouldn't be showing up on infrared.* Approaching slowly, she heard the sounds of fangs tearing flesh. Through the snow, she made out a shape crouching over a sapien body. Red splatter across white fur. The animal looked up at her and growled, its fangs red, its mouth dribbling, yellow eyes bright.

An ice wolf, she realized with disappointment. It moved away from the half-devoured corpse it was feeding on and began to circle her, its back arched, fangs bared. She took aim and fired. The beast squealed as her harpoon caught it in the eye, and went through its brain. It twitched a few seconds before dying. A scavenger, dogging Kral's tracks and feeding on Her leftovers. Not unlike herself. She reluctantly examined what was left of the sapien corpse and saw that it was one of the hunters from the eastern continent. Kral had been busy. And, the odds were stacking up against her. Each death brought her that much closer to finding Zaard. No, she would not think of that.

She trudged to the wolf's carcass and extracted the harpoon from its skull, wiping the blood on its fine fur pelt. She ran her hand across the fur. Beautiful. Soft and white as the snow. A survivor, this one, were it not for sapien interference. She could not afford to waste any time, but it would be foolish to pass up a chance for fresh nourishing meat. Pulling out her knife and hand ax, she skinned, gutted and dismembered the animal, wrapping the meat in the pelt and storing it in her backpack. As she was skinning the animal, she was struck by the grotesque deformity of its genitalia. Then she realized it was no deformity. This was a male.

Saaryth had mused something about that, on one of their long walks on the beach on Keltrys IV, long ago. Sea turtles laying their eggs in the sand had caught her attention. "Have you ever wondered why it is that sapiens are the only higher species that has no males?

The only species that hunts another for its young, instead of bearing its own offspring?"

"Not really," Kaylenn had replied, a bit puzzled at so strange a question. "Why?"

"Some of our scientists believe that our very remote ancestors must have evolved from such dimorphic animals, but chose to genetically eliminate male sapiens and start over with other forms, like Kral and Kaltaari." Kaylenn had laughed at that, as obscene as the idea was. It would have been heresy among her own people, of course, warranting public execution in earlier centuries.

The blood trail led her to the edge of the flow. At the water's edge huge, bristle-faced, comical-looking gray sea mammals flopped about on the shifting ice sheets. One of them looked up at her with an anthropomorphic expression of dull disdain. The animal looked away a moment later, and seemed to yawn. Kaylenn smiled. This was probably the last truly unspoiled place on Zeln, she realized. *Until the Combines find some way to exploit it.* For all its harshness, it was beautiful. Above all, it was clean. Uncompromised.

The idyllic scene was ruined as she came upon the next body. It was becoming irritatingly monotonous. This body looked fresh as she approached it. The dusting of snow was not thick—and the body was whole. Uneaten. It was then she discerned the shaft of a harpoon protruding from the dead feme's back. She dropped and scanned. Nothing. Her enemy might be concealed behind the shoulder of the hill nearby, she thought. She kept her eyes fixed on that hill as she approached the body. Virtually suicidal, she knew, coming out into the open like that, instead of taking cover. But she had to know. She pulled the harpoon from the dead feme's back and slowly began to turn the body over. Something red flickered peripherally across the lens in her goggles, off to her left, on the hillside. She fell face down across the corpse just as she heard the faintest crack in the distance. She shouted in pain as the harpoon cut through her thermal suit and grazed the muscle in her shoulder.

She looked into the dead face touching her own, and saw that it was not Zaard's. She struggled to turn the body on its side, using it as a shield. Another crack in the distance and a second harpoon skewered the corpse through the face, its tip coming out the back of the head and missing Kaylenn's throat by an inch. She scanned the hill, barely catching the red glimmer of her enemy's head signature as it slipped behind the protection of the hill's snowy curve.

She surveyed the terrain. Hopeless. Her enemy had three clear advantages: height, cover, and time. If Kaylenn tried to storm the hill, she would be dead before she took ten strides. If she played this out, crouching behind a cadaver and waiting for a hopeless opportunity of gaining a quick bead on a distant thermal shadow, she would end up freezing to death. The witch probably had a heating unit set up behind that hill, she thought bitterly. She thought of the heating unit in her backpack, but quickly put the thought out of her mind as another harpoon flew into the dead feme's chest. The heat shadow seemed to wave mockingly as it slipped behind the hill.

She was trying to goad Kaylenn into wasting ammunition, obviously. But, the sniper doubtless had an ample supply of her own. Her fingers turning to ice inside her gloves, the wind screaming in her ears, Kaylenn wondered if she could manage to pull at least one of the three heating flares from her backpack. Each would burn for only about ten minutes, but that would be ten minutes. An idea struck her. She scanned the distance to the hill and switched in radar mapping for an exact figure. It would not be easy to run that distance in the snow, but it was better than waiting where she was. The numbness was spreading through her hands. She had to try it.

She dug her legs under the snow, burying herself to her waist and covering herself under the corpse. She slipped off her backpack and struggled through its contents, swearing under her breath, the wretched weight of the dead feme on her back, her shoulder wound stinging in the cold, the snow finding its way into her pack. She tried to shake the damnable numbness from her fingers as she pulled free two heating flares, cut two short lengths of climbing rope and tied the flares to the tips of two harpoons as tightly as she could. She widened the range of her radar scan and boosted its power to the limit of its tiny power cell. *That should jam her radar well enough*, she thought as she calculated the angle and distance for her first and second shots. She loaded the first harpoon into her rifle.

The aim would be the hardest part. *Impossible while sheltering behind this wretched bag of meat and bones. If only that witch on the hill would launch one more harpoon.* It would take her several seconds to reload. That would be all Kaylenn needed. She struggled under the corpse and lifted the muzzle of her rifle toward the hill. She heard the crack of the sniper's rifle. A harpoon lanced through the dead feme's arm, just missing Kaylenn's shoulder. She threw the corpse off herself, lit the first flare and fired. The flare-tipped harpoon exploded in an eruption of glowing red light about twenty feet short of the hill. Kaylenn bounded across the reddened snow, straight into the source of the light. A wave of heat like a summer wind washed over her. She was now invisible on infrared as well as radar. And the sniper would, she hoped, be momentarily blinded by the infrared flash.

A harpoon landed in the snow a good two meters from her. She ran a serpentine course as she struggled to load her second shot. She fired, and the second flare exploded at the base of the hill. She ran up the slope, red light bathing her in delicious warmth, the snow turning to slush under her boots. She reached the top and scanned the hill in the flickering amber light. There her enemy lay, crouched just below her, wrapped in a thermal mat linked with a heating unit. She was shifting her rifle about, searching the slope for Kaylenn.

Kaylenn advanced toward her. A bit of snow was dislodged by her boot and spattered against the heating pad. The feme looked up and swung her rifle toward Kaylenn. Kaylenn screamed in rage as she threw her empty rifle and leapt from the ridge. The sniper knocked Kaylenn's rifle aside, her aim slipping as she fired. The harpoon slashed through Kaylenn's thermal suit, slightly grazing her ribs. She landed atop the other feme and joyfully landed a solid blow across her face. Her opponent retaliated, hitting her across the face with the butt of her rifle. Blood filled Kaylenn's mouth as they struggled. She spat it into her enemy's face, and kneed her in the ribs. Kaylenn knocked the rifle aside and hit her opponent's face again. The other feme tackled her, and they rolled down the hillside together, into deep snow.

She landed a punch to Kaylenn's jaw. Kaylenn's head swam through stars. Her adversary was strong, and Kaylenn's muscles were still stiff from the cold.

Kaylenn's enemy soon gained the upper hand. She pounded Kaylenn's face until it was numb from the pain and the cold, then pushed her face into the snow, her gloved hands strangling Kaylenn until her vision dimmed. Blackness flooded over her. Out of the darkness appeared a young girl, seven or eight, perhaps, with long reddish-blonde hair and blue eyes, reaching out to her. An older feme with sandy-gray hair—a feme Kaylenn remembered seeing once before—held the child back, her hands tightly gripping the young one's shoulders. *You mustn't interfere, Faln,* she dimly heard as they both disappeared.

Icy cold wind blasted into Kaylenn's face as her respiration mask and goggles were torn off. As the blurred image of another feme's face in mask and goggles slowly appeared, she found herself being pulled roughly forward by her tunic. "Kaylenn," her enemy said in cruel delight, "I'm going to enjoy this." Kaylenn heard her draw a knife from her belt. Kaylenn felt the sharp, serrated edge against her throat. She heard a loud, familiar crack nearby. Her attacker's face shattered, blood and bits of smashed goggles splattering Kaylenn's face as the tip of a harpoon slid out the other feme's gutted eye socket. Her enemy fell dead on top of her. She picked up the knife and tried to use the dead feme as a shield, as she had before.

The feme who had fired the harpoon stood silhouetted against the last of the flickering amber light of the flares, standing tall upon the hilltop. "Kaylenn?" she called out cautiously.

"Zaard!" Kaylenn called out joyously, pushing the dead witch off of her and wiping the blood from her face. Zaard ran down the slope and joined her, pulling back her hood and tearing off her mask and goggles. She had never looked so beautiful. They embraced and kissed. Despite the pain of her bruises, Kaylenn was grateful for the strength of Zaard's arms around her, and the soft warmth of her lips. They looked into each other's eyes. "I love you."

"'Sorry I let it get that close," Zaard whispered,

stroking Kaylenn's face with an expression of tearful gratitude. "I had to be sure who was who." They kissed again, fighting the growing numbness with their shared heat. Reluctantly, they strapped their respirator masks back on, and re-fastened their hoods.

"Let's see who our friend is," she said, pulling open the dead one's tunic. The nameplate read Wraand, South Continental Province. "Damn," she whispered angrily. Not Kelnaath. "This makes six down, by my count."

"I found another," Zaard said. "Killed by Kelnaath. This leaves only us, and her."

"Good. Kral's wounded. She'll be close by. Kelnaath will, too, we can be sure of that. It's getting on to night." She slipped Wraand's knife into her boot. "We should set up camp and hunt at first light."

"You're hurt," Zaard noticed.

"I'll keep till we retrieve my pack and get the tent set up." She smiled and patted Zaard's strong shoulder. "I have an interesting meal planned."

Chapter 42

Timeline: Kalthaar Experiment
Timeline Spatial: Near the Heltryth Ice Flow, Planet Zeln, in the galaxy of Kalthaar
Timeline Chronological: The fourth millennium after the age of Kaarth, section point 123120

The wolf meat was not half bad, once cooked ovor the heating grill. A bit stringy, but after subsisting on field rations Zaard was grateful for the taste of warm meat. "You're gorgeous, and you can butcher your own meat," she said with a smile, taking a bite of the meat off the tip of her knife. "As warrior caste femes go, you're not such a bad catch."

Kaylenn laughed, taking a bite of the meat off her own knife. The night wind howled outside, rattling the flimsy plastic surface of their small dome-shaped tent. Wolves howled into the wind, no doubt fighting over the scraps of recent sapien folly. Finishing her meal, Kaylenn slipped under the heating mat with Zaard, pressing her warm body close. "The trip wires are set?" Kaylenn asked quietly, kissing her on the neck.

"All set," Zaard replied, running her fingers through Kaylenn's free-flowing, beautiful red hair. "Nothing will sneak up on us tonight without sounding an alarm."

"Good work." They kissed as they disrobed. Kaylenn winced a bit.

"'Sorry," Zaard said, minding the medical salve she had put on Kaylenn's shoulder. She held her as they sank into warm, sweet darkness. In the course of their lovemaking, as Zaard's mind was lost in the spinning rush of pain and pleasure, her visions were, strangely enough, not only of Kaylenn, but of Saaryth. Of what she was, and what she offered. The hunt of Kaltaari. The strength and comfort of the tribe acting as one.

The many infants. The memory of Kaylenn's courage as she attacked Kral filled her, but it was only part of something larger. The power of All. The light of the One.

Pre-morning gray filled the tent as they lay in each other's arms under layers of clothing and blankets. All was still and cold. The power cells in the heating units had to be conserved. "The sun's nearly up," Kaylenn said.

"I know," Zaard answered, checking her backpack and weapons beside her in the dim light. "Do you think it's close?"

"What?"

"Kral. Do you think it's still close?"

Kaylenn paused. "I don't know. Probably if...if She's still healing, She'll stay close to Her hunting ground, to keep Her strength up." She paused a few seconds. "'It?' I've never heard anyone call Her that before, at least not one of us."

"'Us?' Are we still Kralites? We're violating Primary Law just by being here together, Kaylenn, and by being with Saaryth. Anyway, you don't really believe that animal we're hunting is a goddess, do you?"

Kaylenn raised her head swiftly. "I... I'm not sure." She rested her head back down. "When I was a kid, the priestess at our temple always said the spirit of the Mother/Destroyer lived in the body of Kral, and that the Hunt was Her judgment on us. That that's what set us apart from the lesser animals. I don't know if I still believe that literally, but it does explain a few things."

"And what of the part about Kral's cowardly whore of a sister, Kaltaari. Mother of All Harlots. They say she created the Other to tempt the daughters of Kral with false promises." She laughed a bit, oddly comforted by the foolishness of the old legend. "You actually believe that, too?"

Kaylenn sighed. "Not since knowing Saaryth, and living on Trynn. No. There has to be more to it than what our priestesses say. Still...," she rolled over to face Zaard. "The Kaltaarists, they don't believe anything of the individual survives this life. They believe that when we die, we just melt back into the Cosmic Whole, Its spirit embodied only in Kaltaari. No soul. No goddess of any kind who could care enough about us to assume sapien form. No. I can't accept that. Not after what I've seen."

"What do you mean, 'What you've seen?'"

Kaylenn moaned deeply, stroking Zaard's hair. "You wouldn't believe it."

"Try me."

"I've seen... people. Spirits, I mean. Or, higher beings. Call them what you like, but I've seen them."

"In the flesh?" She was beginning to worry.

"In visions. During the war, in the prison camp where Saaryth and I were held, and here, just before you rescued me."

"Hallucinations!"

"I might have said so. Except that Saaryth had the same visions in the camp, and she doesn't believe at all. She saw the same person I did. A feme with gray hair and strange orange robes. The descriptions matched exactly."

"What?" She was horrified. "Are you playing with me?"

Zaard withdrew slightly.

"No! It's true, I swear."

"Why didn't you ever tell me?"

"I don't know. Maybe I was afraid you'd think I was insane. I don't pretend to understand it. I just know there's a reason for all this."

"Nonsense," she grumbled angrily, rolling over. "There's nothing but what we make for ourselves. Does

Saaryth agree with you about these 'visions' of yours?"

"I don't know," she sighed. "Some of the theories she's put forward to explain it are more fantastic than anything the ancient scriptures mention. But she and I haven't really talked about it in years. Deep down, though, I think a part of her wants to believe it."

"Well, I don't. I haven't been visited by any goddesses. Ever." Thoughts of the Kaltaarist trade mission entered her mind. Then, thoughts of Trayl. She clenched her teeth in anger as the damned tears stung the corners of her eyes.

"When we first met, you hated the Kaltaarists. You didn't believe in the goddesses even then?"

"I wanted to, but it was a lie! A stupid, empty lie, like your damned visions!"

"What's wrong? Why are you so angry?"

"Leave me alone!"

"Love..."

She reared up in anger. "I said-" The scream that followed went through her like a shrieking wind, turning her blood to ice. Something huge ripped through the tent, long, saber-like claws shredding the plastic tarp. The monster's many green eyes glowed like fire through emeralds. Its huge mandibles snapped as it sought its prey. Zaard screamed in terrified rage as she pulled her hand-ax loose from its binding on her pack and swung, putting out two of the beast's eyes.

The animal shrieked, black blood bubbling from the ruptured orbs like boiling pitch. The devil reared up on its four hind limbs and lifted its two curved forward claws. The last of the tent was shredded and fell away. Kaylenn stabbed up into the beast's mouth with her spear. The monster shrieked and sent her sprawling across the snow with a back-sweeping stroke of a claw. Zaard rolled as Kral's other claw stabbed down at her. It sliced through her snow suit and pierced her side, pinning her to the ground. She felt something split inside her.

The monster screamed as Kaylenn hurled her spear like a javelin, grazing its flank. The beast retaliated with a stream of acid spit. Kaylenn leapt aside, the acid scorching the back and shoulders of her suit. Dizzy with pain, Zaard pulled her knife and threw it, putting out another of the monster's eyes. The beast howled and bore down on her, its hideous bubbling face coming toward her, its mandibles widening to crush her skull. Kaylenn wedged her spear shaft between the mandibles and forced them apart. Acid frothed, the metal of the spear beginning to dissolve, acrid-smelling silver liquid burning Zaard's tunic and stinging the flesh on her neck.

"Get off her, you piece of filth!" Kaylenn screamed, dropping the spear and stabbing viciously into Kral's side with her knife. Kral swung her claw with lightning speed, opening a wide gash across Kaylenn's chest and knocking her aside like a bothersome fly. Zaard screamed in pain as the monster pulled its claw from her side, turning to go after Kaylenn. Clutching her chest, blood gushing over her hand, Kaylenn struggled toward her backpack. As Kral closed in on her, its mandibles snapping, Zaard forced herself to move through the pain. She picked up the hand-ax and hurled it with both hands as hard as she could. It cut a deep gouge in one of the beast's hind legs, black blood splattering across the snow.

The creature screamed in rage and turned toward her, unleashing another stream of acid. It fell on her leg, quickly eating through the suit, then through flesh and muscle, like a white-hot iron skewer straight to the bone. Zaard screamed, almost fainting from the pain. There was a blinding red flash and a wave of heat. Kaylenn had set off a heating flare and tossed it directly under Kral's belly. The monster screamed in agony, its open wounds scorched in the fire. It scampered away quickly, clawing its way down the slope and losing itself in the deep snow before Kaylenn could get a bead on it with a harpoon rifle.

Kaylenn pulled a med kit from her pack and staggered over to Zaard, leaving a trail of blood in her wake. "Lie back," she gasped, bending over Zaard and pulling a strip of adhering salve from the med kit. Zaard applied pressure to Kaylenn's wound, stopping the bleeding as well as she could "Lie still!"

"You're losing blood," Zaard protested, fighting to stay conscious through the pain. "You're no good to me dead." She winced in anguish, her ribs feeling like they were going through her lungs.

"Lie back," Kaylenn said, pulling off her jacket and tunic. "In this cold the blood will clot faster anyway." She applied the bandaging, dressed herself, then started on Zaard. "Brace yourself," she warned, probing Zaard's side with her fingers.

She heard something crack, and the pain shot through her. "How bad?" she asked through clenched teeth.

"Three ribs broken. I have to stop the bleeding and stitch you up. Then bind those ribs."

"That devil may come back soon. You're going to run out of flares. Give it up, Kaylenn. Leave me here and save yourself."

Kaylenn looked at her with an expression of disgust. "Shut up."

An hour later, Kaylenn huddled close to Zaard in the small cave she had found, a harpoon rifle trained on the entrance. The sun was rising, a rainbow of colors washing over the ice. The heating unit they were using had barely an hour's worth left in its power cell, and their rations were all but gone. She checked the dressings on Zaard's wounds and found them soaked through with blood. As she had feared, the stitches had not held on the trip up the mountainside, and she had neither the time or material to sew her up again. Zaard moaned in pain, sweat beading on her face.

The makeshift litter Kaylenn had made out of climbing rope and the remains of the tent was firm enough, at least. But the tourniquets were inadequate. Zaard had to be airlifted to a med facility quickly, Kaylenn realized, gently wiping the sweat from Zaard's face. The only way she could save her was by finishing the hunt quickly. "Try to hold on," she whispered, taking her hand and kissing her on the cheek. "Once Kral is dead, they'll have an airsled here in minutes."

"It would be smarter to go after Kelnaath first," Zaard said in a strained weak voice. "With Kral wounded, she's the greater threat."

"Don't argue," Kaylenn said, finishing her preparations. She cursed herself for her over-confidence, looking over the now-useless trip wires she had used to bind her spear, cut cleanly through by Kral's mandibles when She'd come upon them in the tent. The race memory of the beast? Or the cruel cunning of a goddess?

"Isn't this the part where I'm supposed to play Jaeven to your Kaarth," Zaard joked, a thin smile cutting through her obvious agony.

Kaylenn could barely look at her in that state, but she was in awe of her courage. She would not let her die. "As I remember the story, Kaarth was the one injured." She forced herself to smile.

"But Jaeven was the one with good sense." She began coughing uncontrollably, hacking up blood. Kaylenn held her until the fit passed, then wiped the blood from her chin.

"I'll be all right," she whispered, stroking Zaard's fevered head. "We both will."

"I owe you an explanation," she whispered, touching Kaylenn's arm.

"For what?"

"For why I wouldn't believe in your spirit visions, and why I made it so hard for you on Trynn."

"Never mind that now. Rest."

"No. I want you to know this about me. When I was a kid I never cared much about hunting Kralines. I never dreamed about being a warrior, or hunting Kral. I just wanted to be a farmer. The others laughed at me. Called me 'Kaltie.' When I was old enough for sex, there wasn't any. Nobody wanted me."

"They were fools," Kaylenn whispered with a smile, gently ruffling Zaard's hair, and bitterly remembering every servant caste 'coward,' every cleaner and laborer she and her friends had tormented and beaten when she was in her teens.

"When I was about sixteen, there was this Kaltaarist trade mission from Trynn based near our village, and, well, I'd heard things, you know? I was curious. Lonely. So, one night, I hiked out to their trading post. They seemed cold, at first. But I think they could see my pain. They were kind to me. Gentle. They understood. I never thought it could be like that. It was.... Anyway, I was missed, and a couple of the supervisors from my cluster came looking for me. They found me, with them. Called me a little whore and a Kaltie-lover, said I'd rot in the desert of eternal pain when I died, old and diseased and alone. They dragged me back to the village, and next morning, strung me up naked between two poles. Flogged me in front of the whole village until I passed out. They doused me with cold water, and I could hear everyone laughing-"

Kaylenn squeezed her hand. "You don't have to."

"I want to. I want you to understand. They shipped me off to the capital, where I spent a year in a reconditioning center. Neural shock treatments. Beatings. The guards raped me when they felt like it. All of them together. Part of what they called 'aversion therapy.' Afterwards, there'd always be a priestess there, telling me I could survive the ordeal by calling on the strength of a matron goddess. I didn't want to choose one, at first. But then they shocked me and drugged me until I started to see them."

"You saw goddesses?" Kaylenn asked through tears of anguish.

"Yes. Walking off to the Hunt. Tall and powerful in their feathered cloaks, carrying their bows and spears." She smiled, beginning to sound slightly delirious. "I chose Taarex as mine. I always thought she was the most beautiful. Dark and alone, like me. She got me through it somehow. I hated the Kaltaarists for what they'd done to me, and I loved Taarex for making me strong. Then, they sent me home. 'Healed,' but never forgiven. Or accepted. When I was old enough, I transferred to another production sector, then another. But my reputation followed me. Wherever I went, I had to fight to gain respect. I got to be good at it. Taarex was with me. I took pride in that. I always wore black to honor her. After a while, they pretty much left me alone. Then, when I was about twenty, in Zed-4, I met Trayl.

"She was different. She understood. She was so much like me. I felt like Taarex had rewarded me for my strength by sending her to me. It happened right away. She was my first one on one. It was beautiful. We stayed together for years. After we'd saved enough, we started our own farm. Did damned well, too. One of the biggest farms in the sector, we had. We secretly made fun of the fools who went off to war with stupid dreams of glory. Let them fight and die. We had each other and the farm. What else was needed?

"Then the war came to us and we lost each other. I came home to find she was dead. Taarex had punished me for being weak," she whimpered. "Love made me weak. I didn't ever want to love anyone again. All I trusted then was the land. And then someone came and tried to take that away. I couldn't let it go. It was all I had left. There was nothing left to do but fight."

"With Taarex at your side?"

"I didn't know anymore if she was my ally or my enemy, but she'd taught me to be strong, and I would use that to fight for my land and my cluster. To protect what was mine. But I couldn't." She sighed. "It all died around me and I couldn't do anything to save it."

"You fought well. As well as anyone could."

"For all the good it did. Then came you and Saaryth, and I saw Trynn. I didn't, couldn't believe that their way could be stronger than ours, but it was. Their way is better. Inside, I always knew it. I was always meant to be one of them. It's who I am. I can't deny it anymore. I am Kaltaarist."

Kaylenn understood. "And when I told you I'd seen a goddess?"

"I didn't know what to believe anymore. I'm afraid, Kaylenn." She clutched at Kaylenn's arm, her face twisted in pain. "I'm afraid nothing I believe is real. I feel like I've spent my life chasing shadows, looking for the light. Kaylenn, Love, what do you believe?"

"I know I love you. That's enough." She held her hand tightly and looked out at the kaleidoscope of colors washing over the ice as the sun rose. Long shadows of red and orange and purple. "The shadows can point you in the right direction sometimes, if you let them," she said, gently propping Zaard's head up so she could witness the beauty outside. "Light and shadow. Why do we have to choose?”

“The light is forever.”

“Shadows come and go, but we’d be fools not to enjoy them while they’re here. Where there’s light, there’s shadow. We need both. Like I need both you and Saaryth. Why should any of us have to choose? It’s all here for us.” She swept her hand across the colors of the rising sun. “We can use it all as we see fit.”

“What do you think it was that you saw?”

“I don’t know. Maybe, the source of all this. The light, the shadow, all of it. Or maybe just someone else looking for the same answers. I don’t know. I don’t care. I just know I’m going to get both of us back to Saaryth alive.” She gathered her equipment as the sun cleared the horizon and rose over the ice sheet, a bloody, dripping ball of molten gold. She kissed Zaard lightly on the lips. “‘See you soon,” she whispered, and set off across the ice.

Chapter 43

Timeline: Kalthaar Experiment
Timeline Spatial: Near the Heltryth Ice Flow, Planet Zeln, in the galaxy of Kalthaar
Timeline Chronological: The fourth millennium after the age of Kaarth, section point 123121

The wind stung her chest and shoulder wounds as she made her way down the climbing rope into the deep, narrow ravine. The walls closed in around her as she neared the bottom. She found herself in dusky shadow as her boots touched the snow on the floor of the ravine. The walls were sheer, the space confining— and the harpoon rifle all but useless. An attack could come from anywhere, she realized, studying the high snow drifts all around her. She would get only one shot.

The wind howled, distant and mournful. She could hear her own breathing as she loosened the climbing pulley and started her search, her spear at the ready. She neared the snow drift at the narrowest point in the ravine. She approached slowly, her boots crunching against the snow. Kral exploded out of the drift, screaming, an ugly, hateful apparition. Kaylenn pointed her spear directly at the beast and stood her ground, as though paralyzed with fright. As the monster lunged for her, its mandibles opening wide, she touched her belt and pressed the electrical contact she had crudely fashioned using the power cell from her radar scanner. The charge passed through the length of wire linking the makeshift detonator to the heating flare she had fastened to the tip of her spear. The flare exploded in a bright red flash, right in the animal's face.

Kral screamed and backed away. Kaylenn advanced, the flaming spear at arm's length, forcing the animal back against the ravine wall. It tried to escape. She ignited a second flare and tossed it into the snow to block the animal's path. The beast scrambled backward, away from the fire, and she ignited her last flare and tossed it, trapping the demon in a triangle of raging amber fires, penning it in against the wall. Working hastily and awkwardly with one hand, she unfastened her belt, dug two harpoons into the snow, and suspended the spear on a wire strung between them. She smiled. It was over. She had won. "Gotcha, you stupid... animal!" she whispered in glee as she ran a few meters away from the fires and unslung her harpoon rifle.

She looked through the sites and drew a bead on the helpless cowering creature trapped between the fires. So pathetically easy. She fired. The harpoon shattered uselessly against the stone wall of the ravine as Kral leapt to safety. "No," she muttered. *Impossible.* Nothing so huge could leap like that. But it had happened. Its monstrous claws digging into the ice sheet jacketing the wall, the beast climbed the wall, up and out of reach of the fire, moving with the speed of an arachnid. "Nooo!" she screamed, pulling another harpoon from her quiver and struggling to load it into the rifle as the monster turned and leapt for her.

Kaylenn fell backward, her feet tangling in her climbing rope. She rolled in the snow, Kral's claw missing her heart by a split second. The mandibles opened, fetid acidic breath spilling over her. Instinctively, she rammed the barrel of the rifle into the monster's mouth and pressed as hard as she could, screaming in rage as she tried to ram it down the devil's throat. Acid frothed and steamed, dissolving the metal. Kaylenn pressed the rewind button on her climbing pulley. The coils of rope began whipping through the snow as the rope, still anchored to the cliff above, began retracting. The rope tightened around

Kaylenn's ankles and pulled her by her legs through the snow, and out of Kral's reach.

The blood rushed to her head as she was hauled upside-down off the ground and straight up the ravine wall. She heard claws scratching against rock below as Kral quickly scaled the wall, coming up after her. She locked the pulley, stopping her vertical ascent. She reached up and strained, trying to free her feet from the tangled rope. She cursed in rage, swinging like a pendulum. The scratching sound was getting closer. Her flesh crawled, anticipating the feel of acid and claws rending her flesh. Freeing her feet, she twisted her body and swung straight into the ravine wall.

Kral attacked, its claw ripping through her suit and grazing her ribs as she kicked off from the wall. Kaylenn released the climbing pulley and let the momentum of her kick send her reeling out and away from Kral. She quickly locked the pulley, then hit rewind, and found herself being pulled straight toward Kral. If the beast moved again, escaping with that damnable quickness, Kaylenn would be smashed like an insect against the stone wall. She pulled her climbing pick from its ring at her belt and swung it into Kral's back, piercing the monster's tough hide and skewering one of its brain nodes. The animal squealed shrilly, scrambling quickly along the wall in an effort to dislodge her.

She released the pulley and held fast to the pick-ax, still stuck in the creature's back. With her free hand, she pulled her knife and stabbed wildly, first putting out the monster's remaining eyes, then cutting into its remaining brain nodes. Kral screamed so loudly, it almost pierced Kaylenn's ear-drums. The beast lost its grip on the wall and fell, its limbs scrambling in midair as it plummeted thirty feet into the ravine. Kaylenn locked and hit rewind, praying the line would retract in time. She groaned in pain, her back feeling as though it would break as the line went taught and yanked her back up the ravine wall. Dangling in midair, she looked down on the now-helpless Kral, lying flat on its back in the snow, all six limbs thrashing wildly. The screams echoed on and on against the ravine walls, drowning out the wind.

Cho released the pulley and lowered herself onto Kral's belly, drawing her hand ax. She dropped to avoid those thrashing claws, gritting her teeth in anguish as one of them grazed her wounded shoulder. She chopped wildly into Kral's arterial passages, in the exposed areas just below its mandibles. Black blood bubbled and geysered upward, drenching her white snowsuit pitch black. Gradually, the animal stopped thrashing, its limbs weakly twitching until it finally squealed out its last breath and died.

Kaylenn dropped her head onto the dead beast's bulk and sobbed in exhaustion, her head reeling, her body throbbing in pain. *Not a trace of life left in the devil.* The surgically-implanted biomonitor inside the creature would be shutting down now, she realized with joy. They would know the hunt was finished and at this moment would be sending a rescue sled to collect the victor. The infant within would survive inside Kral's womb for those few minutes until a med team arrived and cut her out, placing her into a thermal unit. Kaylenn was not about to wait for that. She had to get back to Zaard.

When her head cleared and her breathing finally returned to normal, she stood, weak and shaky, and hit rewind, the pulley hauling her back up the ravine.

She reached the cave an hour later, and there Zaard lay, under the blankets where Kaylenn had left her. Her head was slumped to one side, as though she were asleep. "Zaard!" she called out, fearfully. "Zaard, it's over! Kral is dead. The animal is dead, and they're coming to get us out of here! Zaard!" *Please, by every goddess...by Kral, because I beat you fairly, and by Kaltaari, because I've learned to love you and your daughters...let her be alive, damn you! You owe me that much at least!*

She heaved a sigh of relief as she reached the other feme and found she was warm and breathing, her pulse strong. *Thank you. Oh, thank you.* "Love? It's all right, now. Here, let me check..." the other feme grabbed Kaylenn's wrist with surprising strength as she reached down to check her wounds. Zaard's head snapped upright, and her hood fell aside, revealing a cruel, gleefully smiling face that was not Zaard's. *Kelnaath.* She drove her fist into Kaylenn's chest. The pain of her wound lanced through her. She dropped just as the sword blade extended and sliced through her suit and across her ribs.

Kaylenn screamed in rage, driving her fist into Kelnaath's evil, smiling face. Kelnaath released Kaylenn's wrist and raised her arm, extending a second blade. She screamed, blood pouring from her broken nose as she lunged. Kaylenn dodged, the blade missed her throat by an inch. She grabbed Kelnaath's arm and flipped her over, out of the cave and into the deep snow. Kaylenn scrambled out of the drift, clawing wildly, the snow reddening with her blood. Kelnaath screamed as she burst from the snow and thrust at her. The blade sliced cleanly through Kaylenn's left ear. Smashing in Kelnaath's teeth with a solid blow, she dropped as Kelnaath fell upon her, forcing her into the snow.

Kelnaath straddled her, trying to hold her in place. Kaylenn held one of Kelnaath's arms down while groping desperately for her knife with her free hand.

Kelnaath lunged for her face and missed. Kaylenn found the knife hilt and pulled the blade from its sheath. Kelnaath broke her grip and freed her arm. She smiled a smile of broken teeth as she crossed her two blades tightly around Kaylenn's throat, the edges digging into her jugular and carotid. One easy double slice and it would be over. "She died slowly," the witch gloated, laughing like a demented butcher. "I made her suffer. She died calling your name! I cut her open slowly, while-..."

Kaylenn put the knife through Kelnaath's eye, and straight into her brain. She was dead before she collapsed into the snow. Kaylenn pushed the dead witch off her, spitting hatefully on her corpse. She saw the rescue sled arriving from the sky to the northeast, its landing jets blazing yellow as it sank toward the ravine. The tears began, and she hated them. They were not enough. She roared her hatred into the sky, emptying her lungs and collapsed, exhausted, into the snow. Only the cold, empty wind answered.

Chapter 44

Faln's prescient vision ebbed. *Kaylenn. Like the sun. Saaryth. Like the ice. Zaard. The rainbow of shadows that passed between them. Brief but beautiful in its ever-changing colors and shades. She would never be whole, neither sun nor ice. Her beauty lay in her anguish.* Ralyn recorded the words into her memory crystal and pressed it into Faln's hands. It would be hers one day. Ralyn brushed aside a tear and kissed Faln on her forehead as the child slept, drained and exhausted in her arms.

Chapter 45

Timeline: Kalthaar Experiment
Timeline Spatial: The Capital of the Northern Continent, Planet Zeln, in the galaxy of Kalthaar
Timeline Chronological: The fourth millennium after the age of Kaarth, section point 123131

Report, Saaryth, Zaalyn's icy voice said in her ear.

Saaryth converted her written report into coded sequence, accessed the offworld comlink and sent the message on its way. A few minutes passed.

Acknowledged. Keep us posted as events unfold. End transmission.

Even through the coldness of her tone, Saaryth could detect an undercurrent of relief. Logging off her private com terminal, she took a deep breath, cleared her mind as she had been taught long ago, in another life she no longer recognized as hers, and prepared herself for what came next. She gathered the necessary documents and placed them in a sealed black leather folder stamped with the Planetary Governor's gold seal. She slipped the folder under her arm, left her assigned quarters and took the lift to the uppermost floor of the Planetary Governor's mansion. Kolis greeted her at the door to the audience hall with two armed guards. "They're waiting for you," she said coldly, her face hard. Zelkys stood at attention beside her in full militia uniform, maintaining a stern, stoic front. Saaryth could see the redness in her eyes.

"I'm ready," Saaryth said quietly, stepping forward. Kolis nodded. The two guards snapped to attention and triggered the security lock. The double doors parted for Saaryth, and she entered the conference hall. Seated around the long oval conference table were the governors of five of Zeln's provinces, excluding the

Northern Continent. Also present was Raast, the Helkos Confederation Chief of State. Raast studied Saaryth from across the table, her keen eyes narrowed and her expression tense. Galactic Press journalists, Combine representatives and high-ranking priestesses stood in the spectator's section, awaiting the announcement to come.

"Esteemed governors, and honored guest." She bowed respectfully toward Raast. "Kaylenn, the new Planetary Governor of Zeln, extends her apologies for not being able to attend this conference, as she is still recuperating from injuries sustained on the hunt. The Governor has authorized me to represent her, and to convey her plans for the new administration of this planet." The five governors grumbled with obvious irritation, no doubt offended at having been met by a mere Kaltie servant. Hardly indicative of a potentially favorable new regime. "First, the matter of who will occupy the chair of Governor of the Northern Continental Province. Kaylenn has selected me to fill that position." She held up the official document.

The room exploded with cries of confusion and protest. "Blasphemy!" one of the priestesses cried. "A Kaltaarist cannot hold sway over the daughters of Kral!"

"I beg to differ, Eminence," Saaryth shouted over the din. "There is nothing in all the history of Kalthaaran law which prohibits a Kaltaarist from serving in an official capacity, if ordered to do so by Kralite authorities. I know of no point of secular or scriptural law which specifies political office as an exception to that rule. So, as I have been selected for this position by the lawfully seated Planetary Governor...the only blasphemy would be for me to refuse."

"Is this Kaylenn's idea of a joke?" cried Myrdis,

Governor of the Southern Continental Province. A thickly-muscled feme with a broad face, short spiked black hair and sharp, angry green eyes.

"I assure you, Governor, it is no joke. If you require a display of military force to confirm the veracity of the Planetary Governor's decree, I'm sure we can oblige."

Myrdis glared at her a moment, then smiled in mocking contempt. "I thought you Kaltaarists didn't believe in violence."

"We don't. Wasteful, like the commercial and ecological policies of the previous administration. However, my people learned during the war that violence can be a useful tool, if efficiently administered. For that lesson, and for your fine instruction, we thank you." Myrdis's eyes widened for a moment as gasps and muttered curses made their way around the table and through the spectators. Raast bowed her head in obvious exasperation. "Furthermore, the Helkos Confederation government has pledged to commit troops to Zeln to enforce its recognition of the new Planetary Governor and all of her appointees. Is that not correct, Your Excellency?" she asked, looking directly at Raast.

"Yes," Raast sighed wearily, glancing up for a second to glare accusingly at Saaryth. "Prime Minister Grath has officially recognized Kaylenn's government." She held aloft the official proclamation document with Grath's signature and the Confederation seal. "Contained herein is the pledge of Confederation military support in quelling any form of insurrection here on Zeln, should the Planetary Governor request it."

"That violates the Confederation Charter!" Myrdis roared in protest, her bulky fist shaking the table top. "Our internal affairs are no business of Helkos!"

"The Council of Ministers disagrees. Zeln has

grievously failed to fulfill on its agricultural contracts, and the Confederation is bound by the Charter's Emergency Powers Clause to use whatever means necessary to claim our property and distribute it for the continued security of our member planets. Accordingly," she held up another official document, "the Prime Minister has approved the following measures proposed to her by Kaylenn. I will allow Kaylenn's representative to explain." Raast leaned back in her chair and relinquished the floor to Saaryth.

"Thank you, Your Excellency." Saaryth opened her folder and read from her copy of the official policy statement which she had herself written and convinced Kaylenn to sign. "Toward the end of restoring Zeln's ecology and offworld commerce, all lands and production facilities currently held by the offworld Combines in all six provinces are to be nationalized, their resources administered toward the common welfare of the provincial populations, minus the compensation paid to the inner worlds of the Confederation toward settling our commercial debts. The provincial governors will now have direct control over their territories and the produce thereof." The other five governors, even Myrdis, smiled broadly at that.

"Outrageous!" a Combine official shouted from the spectator's section. A striking blonde feme with a triangular face and large cold blue eyes, wearing a dark green civilian business suit.

"Unwarranted state seizure of assets," shouted another feme beside the official, probably a legal advocate, Saaryth thought, judging by her crisp black suit and dark eye make-up. "This violates Primary Law, the Home Rule Provision, and several articles of—"

"The Prime Minister invokes the Emergency Powers Clause," Raast interrupted. "The Council of

Ministers has given her its full support. There is ample precedent for government appropriation of private resources for reasons of Confederation security."

"Those precedents only apply in time of war," the advocate objected.

"The Council has spoken. The matter is closed. Any further opposition will be treated as criminal sedition. You will please continue, Governor Saaryth."

Saaryth bowed in false respect. A part of her enjoyed watching her enemies squirm. She could imagine the pleasure it would have brought Zaard, and that tribute, however slight, she owed her. She would not soil Zaard's memory by letting these jackals see her grief. "The second point..." she paused in reading from the text of the statement to allow the room to settle, "as per Zeln's new trade pact with Trynn, Kaltaarist trade missions will be established in the nationalized production zones of all six provinces." The seated governors were silent briefly, their smiles dissolved in outrage and disbelief.

"How large are these trade missions to be?" Myrdis demanded, her face wrinkling in obvious distaste. "My people will not tolerate any sizable—"

"The estimates on cost, production and facilities are available on the terminal screens in front of you, if you will please access the active file," Saaryth interrupted.

Myrdis scowled as she and the other governors activated the terminal screens built into the table top. Their faces went blank with shock. Then, twisted in anger. "Never!" cried Myrdis. "Kaltaarists controlling our industry? Telling us how to manage our own resources! And what is this about offworld labor being flown in from the inner systems? Our industry can't possibly accommodate this huge a labor force!"

Saaryth sighed in fatigue, barely trying to hide her

disgust. "New industries are being brought to Zeln. Rest assured, there will be work for all. Badly needed work." She glanced at Raast and discerned a grudging nod of agreement. "If you'll continue scanning the file, you'll understand the enormity of the undertaking. We are trying to revitalize a dying world. Moreover, a reconstructed Zeln has the potential to become a center for commerce and innovation that will benefit the entire Helkos Confederation."

Most of the officials and spectators looked shocked at the figures and design schematics scrolling across their screens. One or two looked intrigued. "Am I to understand that Kaltaarist medicines and technologies are to be produced in large quantities here on Zeln?" one of the Kralite priestesses asked from the spectator's section, looking up with an angry expression from a hand comp held for her by a young retainer.

"Yes, that is correct, Your Eminence," Saaryth replied coolly.

"I was addressing the Chief of State," the bitter-sounding old cleric snapped. "Not some Kaltaarist whore!" Saaryth actually wanted to smile to display her contempt, but she held her face expressionless.

"The 'Kaltaarist whore' is quite correct, Eminence," Raast said with just a hint of flippancy to her voice. "The terraforming techniques and genetic manipulation technologies the Kaltaarists have developed on Trynn are really quite remarkable, as those reports you've just scanned—reports verified by my own agencies— should make clear. The Kaltaarist proposal put forward by Trynn's Communal Assembly of Planners, if given the necessary Confederation support is, in the Prime Minister's judgment, the only viable plan for the restoration of Zeln, and the long-term revitalization of the Confederation economy."

"Most of the substances and procedures on this list are illegal!" the priestess cried.

Raast groaned. "Illegal and already in widespread use throughout the Confederation, as I'm sure some of the esteemed Combine representatives gathered here could truthfully testify, if initially granted immunity." Some of the spectators gasped. Others laughed. "In any case, the ban on Kaltaarist lore was rescinded, albeit quietly, during the Vedran war, to the benefit of our military forces." She paused, looking pensive. "Given the fact that the Council of Ministers has approved the Prime Minister's emergency powers, I see no reason why the ban cannot be lifted again, for the larger benefit of the entire Helkos Confederation. Now, if there are no further questions, Governor Saaryth will please continue."

Saaryth turned a page in her folder. "The third and final point of the Planetary Governor's policy reads as follows: All financial reparations and material assistance required to facilitate the reconstruction of Production Zone Zed-4 in the Northern Continental Province will be paid exclusively by the Transtar Combine. In addition, Transtar will assume the cost of repatriating all Zeln citizens displaced from Zed-4 by its practices there, should they choose to return. Transtar will also provide interest-free production loans to any and all independent agricultural projects established in Zed-4, provided they are approved by the Kaltaarist ecological and financial planning assemblies. Finally, Transtar will assume all medical costs in Zed-4 attributable to prior Transtar policy. Failure to pay any of these costs will result in total forfeiture of all trading privileges within the Zeln system."

The Combine officials stood silently by, their eyes cold and vacant, their mouths hanging agape. "In anticipation of any further questions regarding that third point," Raast said, the ghost of a smile sneaking across her face, "it will be enforced to the letter. Since we seem to have covered all salient points regarding this transition, and since the Prime Minister's policy regarding this planet is apparently being implemented effectually, I believe that concludes this gathering." She held up a hand, a dam against the flood of open mouths and raised hands that suddenly appeared. "Unless you have something to add, Governor Saaryth?"

"Nothing, Your Excellency. Except my pledge that I will discharge the duties of my office to the best of my abilities, justify the faith that the Planetary Governor has placed in me, and honor my commitment to the Confederation, as I have done before in battle beside Kaylenn."

"Then on behalf of the Prime Minister and the Council," Raast said hollowly, "congratulations and good fortune. May the goddesses smile upon you." She inclined her head slightly, her eyes still probing Saaryth's.

"Then I will make my report to the Planetary Governor, and immediately commence implementation of her policy in my province. I am confident that my five esteemed colleagues will do the same. I imagine the Planetary Governor will summon us all for a summit conference and progress survey within the month. Good day to you all." Ignoring the outraged expressions of the governors and Combine officials, as well as the wild shouts of journalists demanding interviews, she closed the folder, slipped it under her arm, and strode out the door. *For you, Zaard*, she said silently as she walked down the corridor, letting the tears come at last.

Kaylenn sat at the edge of a yawning chasm in the upper reaches of Zeln's northern continent. The cold wind stirred her hair. The primitive necklace she had fashioned from the teeth of the ice wolf she had killed two weeks before clicked as it dangled from her neck. The wind passed in flowing waves across the soft white fur of the wolf pelt shoulder cape she wore.

Saaryth sat down beside her, pressing her body close and throwing a heating blanket around the two of them. "Everything went as we'd hoped," she said quietly, pulling a bottle of Velnyr from her shoulder bag and uncorking it. "There was resistance, of course, but Raast stayed with us. The Trynn missions will begin arriving within the month." She poured the wine into two metal cups and handed one to Kaylenn.

She accepted it, barely feeling the cup in her hand, or its rim against her lips. The wine was bitter-sweet on her tongue. She took a deep swallow and closed her eyes, letting it run like a rush of fire through her veins. Saaryth's head rested softly against her shoulder. "You did well," she forced out, something inside her fighting the spreading emptiness. "You are my strength."

"Let her be your strength as well. I do. The last thing she would have wanted was to become a weakness to either of us."

Kaylenn sighed, holding out her cup. "A part of me died out there," she said hollowly, staring off at the towering white mountains and ice cliffs in the distance as Saaryth refilled her cup. "It felt like my heart had been ripped in two."

"I know."

"Nothing will ever be the same."

"No. But, we have to fight on. As she did. Her life was almost all pain and loss, and she fought on. Not just for herself, but for her people." She cried, kissing Kaylenn softly on the neck and burying her eyes in the softness of the wolf pelt. "We helped her find her way home, you and I. Although her stay was far too short, at least she knew who she was at the end. A part of her lives in each of us now, and a part of her is here." She opened the small environment module strapped to her chest, and under the protective warmth of the thermal blanket, Kaylenn looked down into the face of her infant daughter.

The baby stirred as Kaylenn softly caressed her little face. One of her tiny hands gripped Kaylenn's finger, and Kaylenn smiled, a tear running down her cheek. "Your name shall be Laaryn, my daughter. Which means 'power'," she whispered, remembering a vision from years ago. "I wish Zaard could have held you, even once," she sobbed, wiping the tears from her eyes, "but I will tell you all about her."

"As will I," Saaryth whispered, stroking her finger gently across Laaryn's little cheek, the infant's dark blue eyes looking up at her two mothers.

It was time to go. Resealing the thermal lock on the environment module, they let the baby sleep and carried her back to Saaryth's hovercar. One last look at the distant ice cliffs, then she climbed into the hovercar beside Saaryth. Saaryth signaled the pilot to plot a course back to the capital, and the vehicle lifted off. Kaylenn opened the module and cradled Laaryn in her arms. She felt the infant's gentle breath against her face, Saaryth's arms around her.

Chapter 46

Timeline: Kalthaar Experiment
Timeline Spatial: A remote prison colony on the outskirts of Helkos Confederation space, in the galaxy of Kalthaar
Timeline Chronological: The fourth millennium after the age of Kaarth, section point 123132

Exhausted, Vaaltyr slumped back against the wall of the common area, the smell of the mines fresh on her filthy work coveralls. The weary grumbling of her sister workers—the dross and flotsam of a dozen Confederation worlds—filled the stale air. The smell of sweat and damp earth permeated the dimly lit room. The femes all around her gratefully accepted the meager rations of hard liquor, little more than diluted alcohol, offered them by a feme in military guard uniform. Some went off into darkened corners to take their pleasure from emaciated, drug-addicted whores.

This group was among the 'lucky few' who had met their work quotas and earned such 'privileges.' Vaaltyr refused them. She was no dog licking its mistress's hand for sex and intoxicants. She looked at the filthy rabble surrounding her. Thieves. Street trash. Common derelicts, addicts and drunkards. Products of a once-proud society whose strength and values, whose very soul, were being drained away by Kaltaarist-bred weakness. She was not like them. She had laid down her life for the Confederation in the Vedran war, only to lose her meager job in the metal refineries to cheap, 'efficient' Kaltaarist labor. For speaking out against such corruption, she had been persecuted, jailed, tortured. And now this. But they could not break her. They could not make her forget who she was. She embraced the pain, made it part of her. It made her stronger. If pain offered no fear, then the enemy had no power. This she had learned long ago.

She scribbled her thoughts down as they came to her. She had spent her quota credits on notepaper and simple graphite pens. The guards laughed at the 'great writer.' Stupid blind dupes, the lot of them. Did they not realize they were all being sold out? Led to the slaughter? The guards sat around a small table, playing cards and drinking the same intoxicating swill they gave the miners. A fuzzy hologram image flickered on the tabletop in front of them. Several femes writhing about in perverse sexual brutalities. The guards all laughed. Then, they all swore as the pornography was interrupted by the usual fifteen minutes of state news. Vaaltyr could barely make out the scratchy voice of the newscaster, no chance of making out her blurred features.

"Despite controversy surrounding... zzzzz ...Prime Minister Grath continues to rise in popularity as new employment opportunities continue to arise in the hub syst... zzzzzzz ...following initialization of the largely Kaltaarist-run terraforming project on Zeln. Chief of State Raast denies any allegations of improp... zzzzzzzzzzzzzzzzzzzzz ...Kaylenn, Planetary Governor, and her alleg... zzzzzzzzzzzzzzzzzzz ...controversial appointee to the governorship of one of Zeln's provinces. The first time a Kaltaarist has ever held political office." Vaaltyr got up and walked over to the card table, struggling to hear. "The controversy has bee... zzzzzzzzzzzzzzzzzz ...that Trynn is Saaryth's homeworld. Allegations have been made by the opposing party regarding supposed collusion with the Kaltaaris... zzzz ...ssmbly of Planners on Trynn. Nevertheless, as any of the workers coming to Zeln will tell you, they are happy to be finding gainful empl... zzzzzz..."

Vaaltyr turned away. Numb with shock, she walked into the shadows, surrounded by weak, flickering light. So it had come to this. A Kaltaarist, a filthy, whoring concubine… sat in the office of head of state of a continent while she, a Kralite warrior, labored in filth and squalor on some insignificant mud ball of a planet on the far edge of the Galaxy. They had finally killed her. Yet, she refused to die. Her hate was like a fire warming her cold, dead heart from the inside out. She nurtured the flame of that hate until it grew into an inferno, raging through her veins. She would destroy them. She would slaughter them all, and save her kind from slow extinction. A thundering roar escaped her lungs, and the flow of life around her was suddenly interrupted, guards and workers looking up with a start. Somewhere, she thought she heard a young child cry out.

Chapter 47

Faln screamed.

"Faln!" Ralyn cried, taking her daughter's face in her hands, looking into her panic-stricken eyes. "What is it child? What did you see this time?"

"Fire," she whispered, her eyes wide and staring into emptiness. "Cities burning. Seas of roaring fire."

About the Author

Thomas Olbert is a resident of Cambridge, Massachusetts and enjoys writing sci-fi and paranormal fiction, good films, good plays, spending time with family, volunteering with community groups and long walks along the Charles.

He completed two years of liberal arts college, and is the author of several publications, including Dissent and Holocaust, Books I and II of the Nexus published by Phase 5 Publishing.

Other works have been published by Eternal Press, Mocha Memoirs Press and Lillicat Publishers:

Desert Flower by Thomas Olbert, now available from Eternal Press

Black Goddess by Thomas Olbert, now available from Mocha Memoirs

Anthologies:

In The Bloodstream, and *An Improbable Truth: The Paranormal Adventures of Sherlock Holmes,* now available from Mocha Memoirs Press

Visions II: Moons of Saturn, now available from Lillicat Publishers